WHY IS NOBODY LAUGHING?

YASMIN RAHMAN

D1412919

HOT
KEY
BOOKS

First published in Great Britain in 2022 by
HOT KEY BOOKS
4th Floor, Victoria House, Bloomsbury Square
London WC1B 4DA
Owned by Bonnier Books
Sveavägen 56, Stockholm, Sweden
www.hotkeybooks.com

A CIP catalogue record for this book is available from the British Library.

ISBN: 978-1-4714-1134-2
Also available as an ebook

1

This book is typeset using Atomik ePublisher
Printed and bound in Great Britain by Clays Ltd, Elcograf S.p.A.

Hot Key Books is an imprint of Bonnier Books UK
www.bonnierbooks.co.uk

To my brother, Shamim.
Thank you for always believing in, and supporting, me.
You never accept my gifts, so here's one you can't refuse.

1

'Wassup, everyone. My name's Dexter Murgen, and – fun fact about me – I was named after a serial killer!'

The people in the crowd turn to each other – some with raised eyebrows, others with smirks – but Dexter's not paying attention to any of that. He continues strutting around the stage like he owns the place. And he might as well – he's got them hanging on his every word.

'Don't worry, not a real one, just a TV character,' Dexter adds. 'And the only *real* thing we have in common is our love of doughnuts.'

I watch from my seat at the side of the room and it's weird, like . . . I've seen this set before. I've seen Dexter pace around his bedroom, tracing the exact same path he's walking now, saying the exact same things. We've practised for this stand-up competition *hundreds* of times. And yet today, here, in front of a real audience, it's different. It's new. It's . . . weird. It's the first time I've seen him perform for people that aren't me, people that haven't heard him make dark jokes about his dead mum a thousand times in a hundred different ways.

'I swear I have never seen someone look more uncomfortable,'

Dexter says, finishing his latest joke. 'At least he knows never to make "yo mama" jokes to me any more!' The crowd (if you can call a handful of people in a community centre a crowd) cracks up at this. Someone lets out a hoot and a clap too. It makes me smile. I know how hard Dexter's worked on this set. People think being funny just comes naturally, and sometimes I think it does for Dexter, but I also know from experience how many hours go into perfecting a funny anecdote – making sure it's not too long, that the punchline comes at the right time, that it's universally funny. It's hard work. But Dexter is a master.

And me? Well, I'm the fraud here. Dexter and I have been friends for years, and comedy is the thing that's always held us together. In fact, the first time we spoke, both nine years old, next to each other during a fire drill, we bonded over a joke. Well, I *say* bonded. I started crying after Theo McIntyre said I always smelt like curry and then Dexter made a joke about how Theo had only said that to distract people from the smell of his fart, and that his fart was probably what caused the fire alarm to go off. Dexter's always been there for me since that day, saving me when I needed it. But . . . I can't let him see me crying any more. Can't tell him about the overwhelming sadness that consumes me. Can't tell him what it's like at home. What it's like being me. I can't tell him about any of that. He'd think I was a pussy.

So I mask it. I mask it with jokes, mask it with a fake confidence that I learned from Dexter himself. I mask it by letting him enter me into a stand-up competition that I am definitely not talented enough for. The prize is a mentorship with Kai Matthews, one of Dexter's and my favourite

2

comedians – it's not like either of us could have passed this opportunity up.

I look around the room and can spot some of the people I saw gathering around the sign-up sheet when we arrived. It's mostly guys, mostly in their late twenties, or their thirties. There's no one as young as Dexter and me. Luckily there weren't any age restrictions – that's usually what trips us up from entering anything. Dexter's persistent though. He's not OK with just him succeeding, he's determined to bring me along too. I should be thankful for that, I guess, to have such a good friend, but the truth is, it . . . it terrifies me. The idea of getting up there, doing this, for the first time, in front of . . . so many people. I haven't even told Dexter how scared I am.

The material in my set, a lot of it's about my experience of being a teenage Bangladeshi Muslim guy living in an extremely white town, a white country. It's all, like, a joke, obviously, and it's me making fun of myself, and that seems fine when it's just you and your best mate, but doing it in front of an entirely white group of strangers . . . I worry that it'll make them think it's OK to say the same sorts of things to the next brown person they see.

I keep it safe though – the obvious jokes about terrorism and living with the name Ibrahim Malik, getting 'randomly selected' for security checks all the time, stuff like that. The things everyone says anyway, the things it's somehow become OK to say. I don't go any deeper than that, even though I could. I don't talk about home, about how my parents can't speak English, about how the house always smells of curry, about how ever since I was a kid I've had to basically be a third parent – looking after my two younger siblings as well as being the one who had to talk to the bank when we needed an extension on our loan repayments, sorting out problems with British Gas, trying to deal with adult problems as a puny little nine-year-old. I can't tell anyone about that. Can't tell them about the pressures put on me at home as the eldest child of immigrants. Not even as part of a joke.

I pull out my phone from my jeans pocket. The screen is blank. No missed calls from home, begging me to come back urgently because the Wi-Fi's gone down or they need a babysitter. Dexter makes fun of me for how attached I am to my phone. But he's an only child, also white. He doesn't understand the dread that comes from worrying there'll be an emergency and I'll have to go and sort it out. He has a parent who's capable of being a parent.

I start to worry about the blank screen. What if they call while I'm onstage? What if something happens to one of my siblings and they need me to come and talk to the doctors but I can't pick up the call cos I'm on a stage telling stupid jokes? What if someone dies? It'll be all my fault.

'Thank you everyone, I've been Dexter Murgen, and you've been . . . tolerable! Well, most of you anyway.' He laughs and gives a wave.

The small audience breaks out into applause loud enough to have come from a crowd ten times that size. I push away the bad thoughts and stand up, putting my fingers in my mouth and letting out a high-pitched whistle. Someone in the corner joins in with a holler. Dexter puts the mic back into the stand and does a little bow. He's beaming, and I don't blame him. He was great . . . I think, anyway. I missed the end, because of the bad thoughts, but the crowd loves him, and that's what matters.

Dexter struts his way down the stairs and towards our table, head up, lopsided grin on his face. The same way he walks across the quad when he knows Stephanie Burton is around. When he gets over to me, we fist-bump and I slide his lemonade across to him.

'You smashed it!' I say as he takes a gulp so big I'm sure the bubbles are gonna burn his throat. The bottom of the glass magnifies his grin. There's a shine to him, all over his face, a glow. Part sweat, sure, but also just the pride he has in himself. I wonder how that must feel, to be so sure of yourself, so confident in your abilities.

'Honestly, mate, you were great,' I say. I know he knows it, but I also need to say it. Because it's true. And because I'm a good friend. One who's super proud.

'God, that felt fucking amazing!' Dexter says, smile so wide his teeth glint. He looks around the room, surveying the audience, trying to see whether everyone else feels the same, even though he knows they do. He runs a hand through his dirty-blonde hair – but in a way that's just him trying to look cool, rather than a nervous habit like mine is. As if on impulse, I push my glasses up my nose.

I'm next.

I put my name on the sign-up sheet after Dexter, so that means any second now they're going to call my name. I'm going to have to climb those stairs and . . . speak . . . try to be funny . . . in front of everyone.

Shit shit shit.

'I can't do this,' I say out loud. It slips out as I look around at the crowd, watch people chatter excitedly as they go and get more drinks from the makeshift bar in the corner. I see some of them look over at Dexter, probably talking about him, things he said in his set. This is what they'll be doing about me, talking about me, judging me, laughing at me. Not with me, *at* me.

'I can't do it,' I say again, purposefully this time, looking right at Dexter. I can feel the sweat starting to bead on my forehead.

Dexter looks at me, his expression still happy and smiling. 'And here's the pre-performance nerves right on schedule,' he announces with a laugh.

'No, I'm serious,' I say, swivelling my head around, spotting the judges at their table, seeing them holding the list, looking through it, looking around for me, then right at me. 'I need to get out.' I stand up from my chair, the wooden legs scrape against the laminate flooring, and a woman nearby turns to look. She's judging me, just for a noise. Imagine what she's going to be like when she sees me make a complete fool of myself onstage. I can't do this. I'm going to fail. What was I thinking, letting Dexter talk me into this? He should have known it would end in people jeering at me, in total humiliation. It's all I'll ever be. A joke.

My heart is pounding now, so hard I can feel it all over my body, but mainly in my ears. Thud-thud-thudding. So loud and fast it feels like my ears are about to burst – just start spurting blood everywhere.

'Hey, hey, calm down,' Dexter says. He tugs on my shirtsleeve hard, so that I sit back down. 'Ib, look at me.' I do. He stares at me, wide-eyed and determined. I've seen this look so many times – it's the look he gives me when he's about to deliver a pep talk, about to tell me to stop being a baby, have some balls and stand up and be a man. Do something that's easy as fuck for him. It's meant to be a comforting stare, but I swear I see pity in there too. Every time. Today there also seems to be some anger – he flits his gaze towards someone behind me, gives them a slight head nod and a smile, before looking back at me. I'm getting in the way of his celebrations – stopping him from doing the rounds, celebrating like he should be after a successful set. I bet he regrets being friends with me.

'Ib, you're gonna be great,' Dexter says, taking his hand away, now that he knows I won't move. 'You're going to get up there,' he continues, 'and do the set we've practised five hundred times. You're gonna smash it, and we're both gonna get a bunch of points, right? We're gonna shoot straight to the top of that table, yeah? It's gonna be me and you up there next month for the final. And then . . .' He lets the sentence dangle.

I laugh. This is our practised hype-up speech. We do it every time one of us gets cold feet – which means it's Dexter doing it to me pretty much every time we try anything.

'And then you and me will take over the world,' I finish, with a smile. I roll my eyes and shake my head a little, feeling immediately calmer.

'Exactly!' he almost shouts. 'Murgen and Malik headlining the Apollo, remember? Well, that ain't gonna happen if you don't get up there, right? You got this, man. I promise you. I've heard your stuff. I love your stuff, and you know how hard it is to impress me.'

'Do I?' I ask with a smirk. 'Cos from what I remember, all I need to do to impress you is buy you a Snickers bar.'

His eyes light up, his back straightens. 'You bought me a Snickers?'

I roll my eyes with a laugh.

The echo of the mic static rings out around the room. We both look across and there's a woman standing where Dexter was just a few minutes ago. She's got a clipboard in her hand. The sign-up list. *I've got this*, I repeat in my head over and over. Letting the words take on Dexter's voice because he's the only one that would ever say this to me, the only one whose words I would actually believe. He doesn't bullshit me, I know that for sure. If he says my stuff is good, then it's good. I need to be confident. How the fuck am I gonna be a stand-up comedian if I'm not confident?

Fake it till you make it, right?

'And next up is sixteen-year-old Ibrahim *Milk*,' the lady says, looking at her clipboard, where I've written out my name in block capitals, and yet still pronouncing my surname wrong.

'Get on up there and *milk* it for all it's worth,' Dexter says with a laugh.

We bump fists as I get up from my chair and walk over. Everyone's clapping now, and I keep my eyes down. It doesn't feel as daunting if I can't see them. Maybe when I get up onstage, I can sneak my glasses off. Or I could just stare at Dexter the whole time. Although he might think that's weird.

My body is vibrating by the time I take the mic from the woman, who smiles warmly at me.

'Hi, everyone,' I say, forcing myself to look out into the crowd. Unfortunately it's not like on TV, where the lights are blinding. There's only the ceiling lights in this crappy community centre. Nothing fancy at all, considering it's mainly used for the weekly bingo games and toddler birthday parties.

'My name's Ibrahim *Milk*, apparently,' I say, looking over to the woman, with a forced grin. 'And here I am thinking it's Malik. The opportunities I've missed out on growing up, man.' The crowd chuckles a little. I do the trick Dexter taught me to unfocus my eyes, so that everything and most importantly every*one* is a blur. 'I could've been an excellent mascot for a milk company if I'd known my true surname earlier. Well, *chocolate* milk, obviously.'

I push my glasses up on my nose. 'I could even bring my own glasses.'

The crowd groans a little, with an undertone of laughter.

I go straight into my memorised set, probably speaking too fast, but knowing that if I pay too much attention to what I'm actually saying that I will stumble and lose my place. It takes me a few minutes to get into the swing of things.

'I mean, I have to admit, being racially profiled isn't *all* bad,' I say to the crowd, about halfway through my set. 'At least I never have anyone sit next to me on buses or trains.'

The crowd laughs and I find myself laughing too, anticipating getting the next bit of the joke out.

9

'You suck!' A deep voice rises above the dwindling laughs. 'Get off the stage and go get your eyes fixed, four-eyes!' My gaze focuses. Right onto the table of guys, mid-twenties, a collection of empty beer cans in front of them. They're laughing – mouths so wide I can see one of their fillings. They're mocking me. I knew this might happen. Hell, you go on *expecting* to be booed off the stage right away. But when it *actually* happens, everything you planned to do in response – the jokes you were going to throw back at them, the way you planned to pick out a feature about the heckler and make fun of that right back at them – all that goes right out of the window. And instead of making a comment about how one of the guys has a questionable white stain on his black jeans, you just stand there, frozen on the spot, forgetting your practised routine. It's like my brain has just completely stopped. All I can see is these three guys laughing, heads thrown back, snarls on their faces. The image plays over and over in my mind like a GIF.

My heart is pounding again. So loud in my ears that it feels like it's about to burst. I turn to look at Dexter – he's my anchor – he'll bring it back, bring *me* back. But no, he's fuzzy too. My eyes are focused though! What's happening? Why is my vision so blurry?

Oh.

Oh no.

It's happening again.

This happened just the other day. I was alone in my bedroom, on hold with O2 because Baba had accidentally spent a fortune on mobile data without realising it. And of course I was the one who had to sort it out, which stressed me out so much. Suddenly my heart started pounding hard, my eyes went funny and it felt like I couldn't breathe. It genuinely felt like I was about to die. I thought I was having a heart attack. I was on the verge of calling for an ambulance. Except I couldn't move. It was by far the scariest thing that's ever happened to me. But since it went away after a few minutes, I assumed I was fine. That it was a freak one-off. But no . . . it's happening again.

And everyone is watching.

Oh God, no. They can't see this. They can't see me like this. I need to . . . I need to leave. I look around. Everything is still fuzzy as fuck. I stagger in a semicircle, trying to get away from the lights in the ceiling which suddenly seem to be burning down on me. I stumble, almost tripping over my own foot, and there's a huge laugh from the audience. The panic rises up inside me. Why, oh God, why did I think this was a good idea? Why did I think I could do this? That I was ready for this? That I could handle this?

Someone from the audience says something. A deep voice. I can't hear what, because now my hearing has gone too. It's like I'm underwater and sound can't reach me through the waves.

I need to leave. Get out. Last time this feeling went away after a few minutes. The same thing will probably happen again, right? I just need to ride it out. Alone. I spot a gap through the curtains to the side of the stage. I know there's a small room back there that's used for the women's prayers every Friday for Jummah. The perfect place.

My body feels like it's made out of marble, but the overwhelming need to just NOT BE HERE overpowers that, makes my legs move, makes my feet stagger across the stage and through the curtain. I move as fast as I can down the corridor, and into the back room. I push the door so hard I almost fall flat on my face, but manage to right myself by grabbing on to a chair that's at the side. I sink down into it. I still feel like my body has stopped working, everything inside is broken and I'm about to completely explode or implode or break down.

I feel like I'm going to die.

This is how I felt the last time whatever this pain, this . . . whatever this is, happened. But it went away eventually. I hold on to that thought. It will go away. It has to go away.

Unless it doesn't.

Unless this time it kills me for real.

I'm struggling to breathe. Everything is coming out as a shudder. I pull my feet up on the chair, wrap my arms around them and bury my head in the gap. I focus all my energy on pressing myself together, as if it's up to me to keep myself whole. To stop myself from falling apart. I press myself into a ball, as small as I can, but still the tightness in my chest somehow gets worse, as if my lungs are completely closing. And I realise . . . this is it. This is the end. This is what's going to kill me. I thought it would pass, just a wave of pain, of something more than pain, a wave of . . . whatever. But this time it's worse . . . much, much worse.

This is it.

The end.

2

I reach into my jeans pocket with a hand that's shaky as fuck. This . . . episode, or whatever it is . . . has been going on too long now. Longer than last time for sure. It's something different. Something . . . serious. I need help. I need to call an ambulance.

My hand's barely inside my pocket when sound returns around me, as if my ears have popped. I'm still on the chair, but now I can hear the faint sound of voices from the main hall. Can make out a high-pitched laugh among all that. The fuzziness in my brain disappears. My eyes return to normal and I stop being able to hear every single heartbeat.

Everything just . . . slowly, slowly, begins to calm.

I go to pull out my phone, but as I'm sliding it out, it slips in my sweaty fingers and falls to the ground, skittering onto the gross green carpet.

My legs feel like they're wobbling on the inside, so trying to walk over and get it is out of the question. I reach out – stretching as far as I can while not getting up from the chair that's the only thing grounding me to this room, this place, this reality. The chair tilts slightly, and the phone is almost in my grasp, but just too far out.

Shit.

But then . . . a hand appears. Someone clutches my phone – wrapping their fingers around it and picking it up. I let my chair legs fall back to the ground with a thud and look up to find the owner of the hand standing there, holding my phone out to me.

It's a girl. She's wearing an electric-blue headscarf and a black-and-white polka-dot dress. She looks around my age. She's standing there, smiling at me, holding out the phone. And I'm just staring at her like an idiot.

'Sorry!' I say immediately. I jerk up off the chair too quickly, and then fall straight back down onto it because my legs are still made of rubber.

'Hey, it's OK, stay sitting,' the girl says. She has a nice voice. A soothing voice. The kind they use on adverts for sleep medication or meditation. She's smiling, so maybe she *didn't* see what happened. She wouldn't be this friendly if she had.

I stay sitting, but take the phone from her outstretched hand. 'Thank you,' I say, putting it back in my pocket. I run a hand through my hair and tug at it. Maybe I should just run. Just turn and leg it out of here before things get even weirder. Before she can laugh at me for being such a loser who has weird freak-out episodes that feel like heart attacks. Though, judging by how weak my legs are, I wouldn't make it very far.

'Are you feeling better now?' she asks, again in that medicinal voice.

I push my glasses up my nose, look down at the ground and nod quickly. 'Yeah. I'm sorry, I should have checked this room was empty before barging in.' Although, come to think of it,

14

I could have sworn it *was* empty when I came in. I wouldn't have settled here if I had seen her. Wouldn't have risked anyone, even this stranger, seeing what I look like when I'm doing . . . whatever that was.

'It's no worries, Ibrahim,' she replies.

Wait. She knows my name? How does she know my name? I stare at her, scrutinising her face. She doesn't look familiar, but I've always been a bit face-blind. She's Asian, looks Bengali. Maybe she's a relative? Bridgeport is an extremely white area. Most of the Asians here are some kind of relation to us, even if it's just family friends. Maybe this girl is the kid of some random auntie.

'Earth to Ibrahim,' the girl says in a gently teasing sing-song tune. 'Did you hit your head during that panic attack or what?'

'What?' I ask, voice barely a croak.

A huge grin ignites on her face. 'No one ever chooses "what" when you say "or what",' she says, almost in awe, but with a laugh. 'Kudos.'

'No,' I say, pressing my palms against the chair and pushing myself up. My legs still feel a bit loose, but I clench my muscles, forcing them to hold me up. 'I meant "what?", as in what are you talking about?' I fiddle with my glasses again. I don't look at her face. 'I wasn't having . . . it wasn't a panic attack.'

'No?' she asks, a tinge of sarcasm in her voice. 'So you just . . . *like* curling up on a chair, crying and making groaning noises as you rock back and forth?'

'I-I wasn't . . . crying,' I say defensively.

She lets out a squeaky one-note laugh. 'But you're OK admitting to the rest of it?' She's smiling still. Big, and toothy,

15

and . . . real. She's not taking the mick. She's just . . . I dunno. My instinct is to say she's being herself, but considering I have no clue who this girl is, I guess I can't say that. I want to ask her who she is, how she knows me, and why she thinks I was having a panic attack, but before I can do any of that, she's got something else in her hands. A bottle of water. There's a stash of them in the corner left over from Ramadan prayers last month.

I take the bottle from her. Partly because she's holding it out and it would be rude not to, and partly because I need something to just move the conversation along. I can't tell her that what happened was more likely a heart attack. I can't tell her how serious it was, otherwise she'd make me call an ambulance, go to the hospital. They'd call my parents and then my parents would know where I was tonight. They'd know my secret.

'Thanks,' I say, opening the bottle of water. The room isn't particularly cold, and there's definitely no fridge in here, so I don't know how this bottle of water is as cold as it is. But the feel of it makes me suddenly more thirsty than I've ever been in my life.

'No worries,' the girl says again in her cheerful soft voice as I take a deep glug of water. It leaves an icy trail down my throat, which feels delightful. The girl's looking straight at me. I feel like she hasn't looked anywhere else since I got here. 'A cold drink usually helps after a panic attack,' she says.

My hand jerks so hard a bit of the water sloshes out. 'It's not . . . It wasn't a panic attack!' I say, as a mouthful of water dribbles down the front of my new shirt. 'Why do you keep saying that? That wasn't . . . That's not what happened. I didn't have a panic attack.'

'Why do you get so angry when I say that?' she asks calmly.

'Why do you keep saying it?'

'Let's just say . . . panic attacks could be my specialist subject if I went on a game show,' she says with a smirk.

'Well, you're wrong,' I say, screwing the lid back on the water bottle, so tight my fingers hurt. 'That's not what it was. I don't get panic attacks. I'm not like that. I'm fine.' I run a hand through my hair and tug, look down to see a dark stain on the green carpet where I spilled the water.

I feel a fire start within me. Now that I've pretty much recovered from . . . whatever just happened . . . I'm just confused, angry at this annoying girl for thinking she knows everything. For thinking she knows who I am.

'Who are you anyway?' I ask angrily. But when I look up from the dark green stain, she's not in front of me any more. The room is empty.

3

I turn my head in every direction, trying to see where she's hiding. Why the fuck is she hiding? Did I get too angry at her? Did I scare the strange girl off? I'm just bending over to see if she's under the tables at the side, for God knows what reason, when the door to the room slams open. The noise surprises me so much that I actually fall, my legs losing the trace of firmness they had in them. Luckily I'm still right in front of the chair, so just fall straight into it.

I look up, expecting to see the girl again. Assuming that she somehow escaped and is now storming back in here. But it's not her. It's Dexter.

'Shit, you OK, mate?' he asks, coming to stand in front of me.

I turn my head and look through the door as it slowly closes, hoping to see the girl standing there. But there's no one. Where the hell did she go?

'Ibrahim?' Dexter asks. There's so much concern in his voice that I feel horrible. I shouldn't have run away. He must have been so worried.

'Yeah, I'm fine,' I say, my voice cracking. 'Sorry. I shouldn't have . . . I just . . .'

'What the hell happened? Was it the hecklers? You looked like you were about to faint.'

'I don't . . . I don't know,' I explain lamely. I think back to being on that stage, in front of everyone. 'I started to get these weird pains in my chest, in my arms. Everywhere. I couldn't see, couldn't hear, I just . . . felt like I needed to get out of there. I think–'

'You had *chest pains*?!' Dexter almost shouts.

Oh crap. I shouldn't have said that. Dexter's mum died of a sudden heart attack a few years ago. I don't think Dexter's ever really gotten over how she was here and seemingly healthy one day and then gone the next.

'It wasn't . . . it wasn't anything like that. Nothing serious, I promise,' I say. I hold the bottle of water up. 'I guess that whole "hydration is key" thing is true after all, eh? This water has made me feel all back to normal. I'm *fine*, I promise. It's not . . . it's not like your mum.'

'You can't *know* that,' he says. He pulls out his phone. 'Ib, we've gotta call an ambulance, take you in, get you checked out.'

'Whoa, whoa, whoa,' I say. 'No way. There's no . . . there's literally no need for that. I'm fine, Dex. You want me to say the alphabet backwards? Walk in a straight line while touching my nose?'

He rolls his eyes with a slight smile in one corner. 'That's for when you're drunk, idiot.'

'Well, maybe that's what happened. That woman selling the drinks probably spiked me. She's probably got a bet on who'll win the competition and needed me out of the way. What have we gotten ourselves into, Dex?' I ask it as part of the bit, obviously, but I start to wonder it too. What *have* I gotten myself into? I couldn't even get through one set, and I've signed up for four whole weeks of this. It would be better if this was a thing where people got knocked out at every stage, and they could chuck me out right away, but it's not. We get points every week based on our performance, and whoever's got the most at the end wins. I'm probably on minus points right now, but I know Dexter won't let me just drop out.

'Stop trying to change the subject,' Dexter says. He's got his stern face on – brow furrowed, eyes set. 'C'mon, I'll ask my dad to take us to the hospital if you're so against calling an ambulance.'

He reaches out, as if to help me up, but I jump up off the chair myself. The weakness in my body has now been replaced by adrenaline, or fear of Dexter forcing me to do something that will expose this secret competition to my family.

'Dex, c'mon, don't be stupid,' I say, trying not to let my voice shake. 'It was nothing, I swear. It's happened before, I just –'

'What the fuck, man?' Dexter says. His eyes are wide and full of fear now. 'It's happened before?! That's it, there's no way I'm letting it go. You need to go to the hospital. Or at least book a doctor's appointment. You can't ignore this, Ib. I'll . . . I won't let you.'

I run my hand through my hair and tug at it, force a smirk on my face. 'You gonna unfriend me if I refuse?'

The smirk doesn't transfer like I thought it would. Dexter's face is as serious as ever. 'You know what? Yes. I will cut you out of my life completely if you don't fucking look after yourself. I will drag you down to A & E myself if you don't –'

20

'OK, OK, fine, fine,' I say quickly, imagining the scenario where Dexter forces me into the hospital, where they call my parents, who come and ask what I was doing at a stand-up competition when I said I was going to study at Dexter's house. I imagine the disappointment on my parents' faces when they find out about my hobby.

'No hospital,' I say, forcefully. 'I'll book a doctor's appointment tomorrow.' I move towards the door, hoping me leaving will end this conversation once and for all.

'No deal,' Dexter says, holding his arm out so I can't move past him. He uses his free hand to pull out his phone from his hoodie pocket. 'I'm booking you an appointment right now. I know you, Ib. I know you'll pretend to forget if I don't do it for you. Honestly, I'll have to start spooning your food right into your mouth soon.'

He's already tapping away as I turn back around to face him. I'll have to let him book the appointment and then not turn up to it. He'll never know.

'And don't even think about skipping it,' Dexter adds, not looking up from the screen. 'I'm coming with you. Ah, look, there's one tomorrow, right after school. Perf.'

I guess there's no escaping it now. Dexter's a stubborn git; once he's decided something, there's no way of changing his mind, even if he's wrong – like that time he swore down that our old science teacher, Mr Lipcott, went to jail for selling drugs, when really he just retired.

'There's no way I can come back next week,' I say as we walk home from the community centre. 'They're going to remember

21

what a train wreck I am. They're going to laugh me right out of the door.'

'Well, isn't that the point of stand-up?' Dexter asks. 'To make people laugh?'

'They probably won't even let me in, actually,' I say. 'Not after that. I didn't even get to finish my set. Can they even give points for that? Or is it just automatic disqualification?'

I start to really think about it. Think about what tonight means for my place in the competition, for my dreams of being a comedian. I didn't expect to win or anything, but I had at least hoped to make it through one set. I'd dreamed about that final moment, when people would be looking up at me, their cheeks hurting from laughing so much, tears in their eyes. I wanted that so much. I *still* want that.

'Nah, there's no way they'd disqualify you,' Dexter says seriously.

He pauses, and I feel a tug of affection for him, and his pep talks. For his constant support.

'They can't get rid of the token brown kid, can they?' he finishes.

I laugh and shove him so he hard he falls into a bush.

By the time we get to my house, I'm feeling better. Much better. Dexter has that effect on people. On me, anyway. He says the judges would have told me right away if I had been disqualified. They definitely had the chance to tell me before we left – one of them made eye contact with me and smiled. It was only partly filled with pity. I've just got to do better next time. Work harder. Make it the best set I can do, convince them that I'm worth the time. I just have to . . . make sure this doesn't happen again.

'You wanna work on your next set together?' Dexter asks as we stand at the top of my drive.

'God, yes, please.'

'Now?' he asks. 'I don't have to be back for another –'

'No, no!' I say, probably a bit too quickly, too desperately. I push my glasses up my nose and look away from him, towards the house, where the living-room light is on. 'I need to . . . uh . . . I um . . . should probably, rest, right?'

I immediately feel like shit, as a wave of worry passes over Dexter's face. I'm such a bad friend, reminding him of his dead mum. Using his fear to prevent him coming into our house. Avoid having him walk in and smell whatever curry Ma cooked earlier. Avoid having him try and make small talk with my parents. Avoid having him hear their stilted attempts to reply in English.

Dexter's only met my parents once. I was in the supermarket with them, and he bumped into us. He introduced himself politely, saying hi, asking my parents how they were, while I just stood there sweating so much my T-shirt had great big wet patches.

Dexter's face changed as soon as my parents started talking back. Or at least *tried* to talk back. His smile faded away, replaced with discomfort. So much discomfort. He didn't know what my family is like. Still doesn't know the extent of it really. None of my friends do. None of my friends ever can. It would be the same situation as that meeting in the supermarket, where we all just stood there, waiting for the moment to be over.

'Yeah, rest. Good idea,' Dexter says. 'Text me later? Let me know if you have any more pains. I'll come with you to the hospital – you know that, right? I know I hate hospitals, but if you need someone there . . .'

'Yeah,' I say, ducking my head. I want to tell him I appreciate it. That I appreciate him. But it's weird. It's not something I can actually *say* to him. He'd take the mick. He'd get uncomfortable. *I'd* get uncomfortable. That's not what our friendship is about.

So instead, we just fist-bump before I turn and walk up to the door, fiddling with my keys until I know Dexter's out of sight and I can walk in safely.

4

'Bhaiyya!' my little sister screams for me from her room as I pack her lunch in the kitchen. (Cheese-and-pickle sandwiches, with just the right amount of pickle, and cheese that can't be too thick or she'll cry.) 'Do we have any rice? I need to take some to school.'

'Rice?!' I shout back. 'Why do you need rice for school?' I want to make a joke about what a stupid question this is, asking an Asian household if they have any rice. Mariyam may only be seven, but surely she's seen the giant bin full of rice we have in our storeroom. She must have noticed the way our parents get overexcited whenever there's an offer on sacks of rice at the supermarket, as if they've won the lottery.

'I dunno!' she replies. 'Miss Tooke just said to bring some!'

I roll my eyes, cutting the crusts off her sandwiches.

The morning routine always lands on me. Ma stays up late, knitting, of all things. She says that it's her way of relaxing, and she doesn't get to do it during the day because of chores. So she sleeps in in the mornings, which is fair enough, considering all she does. She used to be the one doing all this until she realised that I could take care of it, and I knew all of Mariyam's fussy requests better than her. And Baba? Well, men are never expected to help out with the housework in our culture, so he sleeps in too. And then the only one left, of course, is me, the third parent.

'Bhaiyya!' another voice calls before I can go to get Mariyam's rice. Hamza's voice has just broken, so whenever he speaks it's always squeaky and weird. Normally it makes me laugh, but I'm too stressed to laugh now. 'Where's my football kit?'

'I don't know!' I shout back.

Next thing I hear is his feet stomping down the stairs, and then he's standing in front of me as I throw Mariyam's crusts away.

'Didn't you wash it?' he asks me angrily. 'I told you to wash it the other day.'

'Ma does the washing – ask her,' I say, feeling the rage rising inside me.

'It's my *football kit* though,' he says, similarly angry. 'You always wash my kit before a game. Remember last time Ma did it? She put it on the wrong setting and it was all crinkly for my match.'

'Well, you should have reminded me,' I say, feeling a pang of guilt. I remember how annoyed Hamza was when that happened. The other team made some horrible jokes about him. I offered to take over after that, but honestly, how am I supposed to remember so many little things?

'And anyway, you're thirteen now,' I say as I click Mariyam's lunchbox shut. 'You should know how to put a wash on.'

'But you SAID you would do it!' Hamza shouts like a toddler. 'I have a match today! Coach already thinks it's weird Ma and

Baba never come to a game. If I turn up in dirty kit, they'll probably call social services!'

'Fine, whatever,' I say, just wanting the argument to be over, for him to leave me to making lunches so I'm not late for school. 'I'll put it on before we leave. You'll just have to pick it up at lunch.'

He groans dramatically and stomps out of the room, muttering about how useless I am.

Baba comes down the stairs and into the kitchen, putting the kettle on to make himself a cup of tea. He yawns, and mutters something to himself in Bengali about being woken up by shouting. As if on cue, the shouting starts up again upstairs, Hamza telling Mariyam to stop screaming, Mariyam telling Hamza to stop stinking. I look to Baba, expecting him to tell them to be quiet and get ready for school, for him to do what a parent *should* do in this situation. But Baba doesn't even seem to hear the shouting. He just pulls out his favourite mug and drops a teabag in it, yawning again as he does. I feel a flash of anger inside me. Striking up among the anxiety and frustration that comes every morning from me trying to wrangle the others into a state where we can all go to school. And all the while Baba just moseys about making himself tea. Does he even know that Mariyam needs her cheese cut the exact right thickness or she'll cry? Does he even hear the arguments that happen between Hamza and Mariyam every single day because she keeps leaving her toys out and Hamza keeps stepping on them? Of course not. The only thing my parents take an interest in is our studies. They know what subjects we're doing and what marks we get, but they'll never ask how we *feel* about them, or who our friends are. They don't pay attention to our lives outside of school. Obviously they don't know about my comedy stuff, and only acknowledge Hamza's football because he walks about in his uniform and gets mud everywhere.

But they should know this stuff, right?

They should pay attention. They went through it all with no help when I was a kid. So they should know. When I was Mariyam's age, Ma made my lunches. Well, she *did*, until one time she sent me in with some leftover biryani and I got made fun of so bad that I begged my teacher to switch me over to school lunches.

One time, when I was like, ten, I slept over at Dexter's house (God knows how I managed to get my parents to agree to that). In the morning his mum made us a huge breakfast spread. Pancakes with fruit, cereal and toast too. Three different breakfasts in one. I was so shocked. I hadn't realised before then that this was what life was like for everyone else. That this is how things were supposed to be. Mothers making breakfast for their children. Not their children making breakfast for the other children.

I'm mostly used to being a third parent now. Become used to the fact I have to do things that everyone else's parents are able to do, that all other adults are able to do. Mostly I've accepted that this is our life, our family, and that I should just get on with it. But sometimes . . . sometimes it sucks. Sometimes it makes me so angry. Like when Baba sees me doing three things at once but doesn't even offer to help.

'Bhaiyya, I need rice!' Mariyam yells again. She's at the top of the stairs now, so I can hear her better.

'Just get some out of the rice bin!' I tell her. She stomps down the stairs and into the storeroom. She's going to make a mess. I know it. I just . . . don't have it in me to care at this moment. I still need to finish her lunch and then pack it, before finding something for myself. Hamza says he's too old to have packed lunches any more. He's going through that annoying early-teen phase. But whatever – one less lunch for me to make, I guess.

The kettle whistles and flips off just as I get out the butt-end slice of the bread to make my own lunch.

'Oh, Ibrahim, I need you to do something,' Baba says all of a sudden. The first words he's said to me today.

'What is it?' I reply in Bengali. I don't say I'm busy right now. That in fact I could do with *his* help. I don't ask if it can wait. Because that's not how things work in our family.

'There's a letter . . .' he mutters, scrabbling through the drawer in the kitchen we have dedicated to important post.

My heart spikes as he rustles, wondering what it could be that he needs my help with. It must be serious. Maybe it's a doctor's appointment for Ma. She was recently told that she's pre-diabetic. Maybe it's got worse. Maybe she needs medication. Maybe –

'Oh, here it is!' Baba says triumphantly, pulling out an envelope and handing it to me. 'The water bill needs paying.'

'Can I do it after school?' I ask, looking at the clock that says we need to leave in the next five minutes if we all want to be on time.

'No, no, now,' Baba says, a smidge angrily. 'They said to do it immediately, or else –'

29

'They only say that to scare you,' I tell him as I throw my own roughly made lunch into a sandwich bag.

'Ibrahim,' Baba says. Stern. Authoritative. Like an actual parent. 'Just call them up now. It won't take long. Hamza can drop Mariyam off at school. Hamza!' Baba walks out of the room, and I soon hear groans coming from upstairs. I feel, of all things, guilty. Guilty that Hamza has to do this now. Do something that's my job. Guilty that I can't do both things at once. But then comes the anger that Baba should be doing this himself. That he should have already taken care of it, considering that this letter came over a week ago, according to the date stamp. The calls for 'urgent last reminder' are probably meaningless now. I'm surprised they haven't cut off the water supply already. But still, I take out my phone and dial the number.

I look at the clock on the microwave, see it tick over a minute, just as the automated voice on the phone says, 'You are caller number twenty-one.'

Yeah, there's no way I'm getting to school on time.

5

I should have known better than to expect Dexter to have forgotten about my doctor's appointment for whatever happened last night at the community centre. I should know by now that any time you mention the words 'chest pains' to Dexter, he freaks out completely and he's not going to let it go. I shouldn't have mentioned it at all. Thinking back on it now, I can't remember whether the pain in my chest was even that bad. It was mostly just pressure all round, and the whole not-being-able-to-breathe-properly thing. Plus the pounding heart. No big. Nowhere near bad enough to need a doctor, but there's no way Dexter's going to listen to my excuses, and to be honest, considering how his mum died, I can understand why. As much as I hate it, I get it.

'See, look!' Dexter says, pointing at a poster on the wall in the waiting room. '*Missed appointments cost the NHS millions of pounds a year.* You would have wasted the NHS's money if you hadn't turned up. You can't do that to the NHS, you heartless bastard.'

I roll my eyes as I take off my blazer. It's suddenly getting warmer and warmer in here.

'Isn't it worse to waste the doctor's time with this? It was just a twinge, just a bit of pain and weirdness. It's not happened since. There's obviously nothing wrong with me.'

'That's what we said about Mum,' Dexter says, his voice deep and fake serious. 'And look where that got her. Scattered into the water like . . . like . . .'

'Breadcrumbs for ducks?' I offer.

'Like breadcrumbs for ducks!' Dexter sits up straight, grins. 'I'm gonna steal that for the competition.' He gets out his phone, starts typing. 'God, the reception is awful in here. I can't even get onto my Google doc. Who doesn't have free Wi-Fi these days? Cheapskates.'

'Probably because of all the money they lose from people missing appointments because they don't have a pushy best friend,' I reply.

The tannoy clicks on. That little click and buzz that sends a jolt of fear through my body. It's the not knowing if they're about to call you or someone else. The worry about whether you should start preparing yourself, and then feeling stupid for lifting your butt off the chair in preparation to walk into the doctor's office when it's not your turn. This time, luckily, it *is* my name they call. I'm up off the chair right away. The other people in the room stare at me, wondering why I'm so eager. They don't get that it's more like an automatic response.

'Want me to come in with you?' Dexter asks, not looking up from his phone.

'Yeah,' I say. 'Actually, wanna go in there and pretend to be me instead?'

He still doesn't raise his head. 'Get me some Nutella for my face and I'm on it.'

I fake-gasp. 'That's super offensive, dude.' I pause. 'You know I'm more of a dark chocolate.'

He snort-laughs as I walk off.

Dr Stenhouse, a young-ish blonde lady with a music-note tattoo behind her ear asks me to tell her why I'm here and exactly what happened yesterday. And as stupid as I feel doing it, I worry more about wasting her time, so I tell her properly. I tell her how I was on the stage, doing my set. I tell her how my chest started to feel super tight, how it felt like I couldn't breathe. I tell her about how my mind went all foggy, and I started sweating. About how I felt like I was going to die. I tell her I'm worried I had a heart attack. That I think there've been a few more twinges in my chest today.

I don't mention the girl I found in the back room. How she suddenly disappeared. I'm still not sure whether she was real or a hallucination.

'Heart disease runs in my family,' I tell Dr Stenhouse. 'And obviously, being South Asian, there's a higher risk of that sort of thing,' I say, remembering all the warnings given to my parents whenever I came to the doctor with them. 'So, I just . . . thought I should come and get it checked out.'

Dr Stenhouse nods through everything I say. It seems forced, as if she's just humouring me.

'Well, yes, you did the right thing by coming,' she says eventually, after I finish my awkward rant. 'It's always best to get these things checked out. Though of course you are

33

incredibly young, and I would be surprised if there was an issue with your heart. You seem fit and healthy. Any other problems before this one situation?'

I shake my head. 'Not really. The same thing happened once before though. Like, the same symptoms as this. A few weeks ago.'

'Interesting.' Dr Stenhouse nods, in that way that our RE teacher does when someone says they believe in something batshit, knowing they can't call them out on it. 'Tell me about that time. What were the circumstances?'

'Umm . . .' I probably shouldn't tell her about having to make simple phone calls for my parents, right? She'll judge us, probably just think 'these bloody foreigners'.

'I was . . . on the phone,' I say. 'Just, in my room, nothing special. And then all of a sudden I got that weird feeling. My heart started pounding, my head went all foggy and I felt like I was gonna die. I think there was that deep pain in my chest again. I don't . . . I don't really remember.'

Dr Stenhouse pauses for a second. Looks right at me. 'What were you feeling before this onset of symptoms? Do both episodes have anything in common?'

'Well, I don't think so . . . ?' I say, getting annoyed by how useless she is. Shouldn't she be checking my pulse or something? 'I mean one time I was at home in my room, and the other I was on a stage at the community centre.'

'May I ask what the phone call was about?' she asks. 'Was it a stressful conversation? Something that made you worried, anxious, scared?'

I suck in a breath. How the hell did she know that? Even if

34

she *is* a mind reader, I can't tell her I was worried about Baba not getting refunded after watching too many videos using his data instead of the Wi-Fi. Can't tell her it was all because of this conspiracy he heard about from one of his colleagues about how supermarkets are selling 'plastic rice'. And definitely can't tell her about how Baba went crazy trying to sift through the bin full of rice we have in the storeroom while I sat on hold to the phone company.

'I only ask,' Dr Stenhouse says after I've been silent for too long, 'because I'm wondering whether this problem isn't to do with your heart at all.'

'What do you mean?' I ask, pushing my glasses up my nose.

'The symptoms you're describing closely match those of a panic attack. Have you heard of those?'

My heart spikes. Those words. That phrase. It's what . . . That's exactly what the girl in the community centre called it. But she was wrong, right? There's no way . . . I'm not . . .

'It wasn't a panic attack,' I say, a bit too forcefully.

Dr Stenhouse's eyebrows rise. She looks right at me. 'What makes you say that?'

I run a hand through my hair and tug on it. 'That's not . . . It's . . .' I take a breath. 'Panic attacks are what people who have mental illnesses get. That's not me. I don't . . . I don't have that. I'm not crazy.'

'Well, firstly, *crazy* isn't a term we use. It's really not helpful.' She stares at me hard, like Mr Wimble does when I purposely say 'orgasm' instead of 'organism' in class. 'Secondly,' she continues, 'panic attacks don't *just* happen to those with a mental illness. They can happen to anyone when they're in a stressful situation. Or even just for no reason at all. Panic attacks don't always have a cause. And they're nothing to be embarrassed about, Ibrahim.'

I feel sweat start to bead on my forehead. My heart starts pounding and I'm worried it's going to happen again. That I'm going to have another episode . . . another . . . panic attack? Right here and right now. Some first impression that would make.

'And thirdly,' Dr Stenhouse continues before the feeling inside me gets any stronger, 'we haven't spoken about your mental health yet, so we can't rule out the possibility that this *is* linked to something going on there.'

I shake my head. 'No. I don't . . . I don't think it's anything to do with that.' The sweat is everywhere now. All through my hair, down my neck, down my back. 'Can't you just check my heart? The pain was mostly there. I . . . I googled it, and it suggested something called . . . angina?' I don't tell her that Google also suggested panic attacks. Three people now (if you count Google and the random, possibly hallucinated, girl) have suggested this. I know this should make me believe it more, but I can't. I just . . . can't believe that's what it was.

Dr Stenhouse stares at me, as if she's going to push the subject, keep trying to get me to talk about my feelings. I will straight up run out of here if she does that. Eventually she just nods a little and then sits back in her chair. I hadn't noticed how far she was leaning forward to talk to me. 'Right, let's have a listen to your chest then.' She picks up her stethoscope.

Dexter's still sitting in the same place when I walk back out to the waiting room. He's the only one there now, and he's slouched in his chair, tapping away on his phone. He looks up when he sees me coming.

'You done?' he asks.

I nod. 'Yeah. Let's go.'

'Thank God,' he says, getting up from the chair and stretching. 'There's no reception in here. I've been playing fucking bridge.'

I pause, look at him with a cocked eyebrow. 'Where the hell did you learn how to play bridge?'

He shrugs. 'It's pretty easy once you play it enough. Plus it's the only app I have that doesn't need the internet.'

'You know that bridge is usually played by old ladies, right?' I adjust my backpack on my shoulder as we walk towards the exit.

'My target audience. They make the best friends. That's why I like you, mate.' He elbows me with a laugh as we open the door to the outside. The air hits my face and I take a deep breath, just enjoying the freshness and slight chill of it compared to how stuffy the doctor's office was.

'So c'mon, spill,' Dexter says as we start walking home. 'What did the doctor say? How's the heart?' He's a bit more serious now, and even sounds a bit . . . nervous?

'Yeah, everything's fine,' I say quickly. 'She listened to my heart and lungs and all that shit. Said there's nothing to worry about.'

'So what happened yesterday?'

I shrug, even though Dexter's looking straight ahead. 'She said it was probably just . . . stress.' I don't mention panic attacks. Dexter would take the piss. Tell me I'm being a pussy, getting panic attacks over a stand-up competition. Getting like that over the thing I say I want to do with the rest of my life. He'd think I was weak, a loser. He'd call me crazy.

It's not true, anyway. None of it. As much as Dr Stenhouse tried to get me to say that's what it was, no matter how many mental-health questionnaires she tried to get me to fill in, no matter how many follow-up appointments she tried to get me to book, I know deep inside that that's not what this is. She's wrong. Google is wrong. The random girl from the community centre is wrong. I'm fine.

There's nothing wrong with me.

6

'You wanna workshop some new material?' Dexter asks when we reach my street. 'The lack of internet at the doctors' got my creative juices flowing.'

'Yeah, sure,' I reply. Then I notice that Dexter's looking towards my front door, and that he probably means right now. At my house. In front of my family. The ones who have no clue about my love of comedy. The ones who, if they found out, would think I was crazy for wanting to make a career out of something so impractical. The ones who would embarrass me in a million different ways in front of Dexter without even trying. 'FaceTime later tonight?' I say, before he can suggest anything concrete.

'Oh,' he says, probably annoyed. 'Yeah, cool.' He pauses for a second, puts his phone in his pocket and then looks at me. 'You sure you wanna carry on with the competition? If that's what's causing you to . . . freak out . . . or whatever –'

'I didn't *freak out*,' I say, a bit too sharply. 'It was a one-off thing. That's . . . that's what the doctor said. I'll be fine. I just . . . I need to practise.'

I'm scared he'll push back on it, tell me I should give it up, rather than risk a repeat of last night. But this is Dexter. He knows how much this means to me.

'I really need to make sure my next set is amazing,' I add, forcing a smile into my voice. 'I'm probably way down in the points. Gotta show them I'm not a joke.'

He smiles. 'You'll blow them away,' Dexter says.

'Hey, leave the terrorist jokes to me, yeah?'

We fist-bump before he carries on the few streets down to his house.

I put my key in the door and turn. Ma's on me before I've even closed the door behind me.

'Where have you been?' she asks in Bengali. Her tone is impatient, angry.

'Just . . . out with a friend,' I tell her. I know if I told her I was at the doctors', she'd be less angry, but she'd worry too, and I don't want her to worry. Most of all, I don't want to have to tell her why I had a doctor's appointment in the first place. She'd ask what happened, and I wouldn't even know how to explain what panic attacks are in Bengali. Not that that's what I had.

'The plumber came early,' she says, pinning me with her stare. 'Your baba was out. It was just me and Mariyam. We couldn't . . . I couldn't . . . explain what was wrong with the bathroom tap. He didn't understand. I tried calling you. Why didn't you pick up?'

'What?' I say, adrenaline flooding my body. 'My phone hasn't rung once.' I quickly take out my mobile, scroll through manically. I would have heard it ring. My ears are always tuned to listen for my phone ringing. For situations exactly like this.

'Ugh, it doesn't matter,' Ma says. Her voice is laced with disgust. Distrust. Hatred.

I would have heard. If it had rung, I would have heard. It didn't ring. It's not even in my missed calls. But . . . she said she rang me. She wouldn't lie.

It hits me then. The doctors' surgery had no reception. Dexter moaned about it. Crap. I shouldn't have gone. It was a terrible idea. It. Just made things worse for Ma, for everyone at home. It's my fault. It's all my fault.

'You'll have to call him and ask him to come back,' Ma says. 'He already took some money though, so tell him he needs to fix it for free.' She stares me down, and my heart pounds under the weight of it, under the weight of being responsible for this problem that's fallen on our family. Also with the anxiety of having to call the plumber and ask him to come back without charging.

'I'll call him,' I promise Ma, dreading the chore already. 'I'll . . . sort it.'

She gives me one last angry look before turning away from me. 'I'm going upstairs. I think he made the tap worse, so there's probably another pool of water under the sink already.' She stomps off up the stairs.

Fuck. Fuck fuck fuck. I hate this. I hate that look on her, and how it makes me feel. I should have been here. I should have . . . I'm always here. Always ready for emergencies like these. The one time I'm not . . .

'I tried . . .' Mariyam pipes up quietly from the living room. I turn to look at her – she's sitting cross-legged on the sofa,

41

TV remote in her hand. She's looking down, and her voice is so quiet.

'Tried what?' I ask her softly.

She looks up at me, and there's a giant frown on her face. It's not like Ma's, where she was mad. Mariyam is just . . . sad. So sad. It breaks my heart seeing her like this.

'I tried to tell the man what was wrong,' she says. 'But I couldn't . . . I couldn't understand what Ma meant. I didn't know how to put it into English. I didn't know what to tell him. I tried, Bhaiyya, I did. I promise.'

I should go over to her, tell her it's OK. I should soothe her pain, like a big brother is supposed to. Like any decent person would do. But I can't move. I can't say anything. There are just bad feelings rising up inside me.

There's always been a language barrier between us siblings and our parents, considering we've grown up speaking mostly English. But Mariyam has it the worst, since the only people in her life that speak Bengali are our parents. Even I speak to her mostly in English. And if there are phrases Ma uses that even *I* don't understand, then what chance does she have?

I'm the one who deals with things like this plumber. This is my role. Not Mariyam's. Me being selfish, going off to do something for me, is the reason she was put in this awful position. I'm the reason she's upset. I'm the reason Ma is angry, having to keep mopping the bathroom.

The panic is rising further and further. It's up to my neck, choking me. It's filled my lungs already, and my breathing has . . . stopped.

Just flat out stopped.

I can't . . . I can't breathe. My heart is pounding so hard it's about to force its way out of my chest. Flop about on the floor until I fall lifeless on top of it.

It's happening again.

The episode.

The . . . not a panic attack.

Definitely not a panic attack.

Just bad feelings. Just anxiety. It's . . . wait, I can stop this. I can control this. I can. It's not a panic attack. It's not. I can fix this. I just need to make myself stop feeling like this. Make the feelings go away. How do I make the feelings go away?

The last two times it happened, it stopped eventually. But I can't wait for that. I can't wait. If I wait, it'll have control of me. I need to be the one in charge.

Water!

That girl in the community centre gave me a bottle of water when it happened yesterday, and it made me feel so much better. That's all it is. I'm probably just dehydrated. *Not* having a panic attack.

I stumble into the kitchen, the bad feelings reaching my eyes now, blurring my vision. I knock into the bar stool and it crashes against the tiled floor. I ignore it. Keep moving, keep heading to the sink. I grab the closest glass – Mariyam's *Shimmer and Shine* plastic cup. With shaky hands, I turn the cold tap on. I run it on full and hold the glass underneath it, making the water spray everywhere. Some of it pinpricks onto my forearms, reminding me that I'm not as numb as I feel. The glass begins to overflow, and I leave the tap running as I guzzle the cold water.

43

I drink it so fast it leaves an icy trail down my throat, all the way to my stomach. I focus on that feeling. The ice inside me, the coldness coating my insides. I focus on that as I gulp and gulp.

The bad feelings don't go away.

I'm panting now, barely able to breathe. I can't help myself from sliding down to the floor, curled up next to the cupboards, hoping to God no one comes in and sees me.

I can't move now. I just have to stay there and wait for it to pass.

I was wrong.

I can't control this.

7

There's a bigger crowd tonight. Even the reception hall is filled with people. Although that might be because the scoreboard is here, with all the contestants' names, and next to them . . . the three judges' scores for their sets from the first stage of the competition. There's a circle of people around it; some of them I recognise from last time.

'C'mon.' Dexter nudges me. He starts approaching the board, but I'm stuck at the door. My feet won't move. I know I'll be at the bottom. I know there'll be a big fat zero next to my name. If I go up and see it, if I squeeze myself through the people and look right at the names and numbers . . . it becomes real. It becomes inevitable that stand-up isn't for me. That I'm not made for the world of comedy. And then what? What else have I got in my life?

Before I know it, Dexter's behind me, pushing me along with one finger in my back. He knows there's no way I'll go willingly. The people at the front of the crowd go into the main room, so the area thins out a little. My heart starts thudding again, the kind of thudding that makes me a bit light-headed.

'Yessssss!' Dexter hisses when we're in front of the scoreboard.

My eyes immediately go to the bottom of the list, not ready to face the truth, but also unable to stop myself.

The name at number ten isn't mine.

'Who's Marshal Erick?' I ask Dexter.

'Oh God, don't you remember?' he says, turning to me. He's got a grin on his face that says he must have scored high. I'm a terrible, selfish friend who didn't even bother to check where he was ranked. 'He was the guy who spent his whole five minutes talking about different types of fish.'

'Oh yeah!' I say, a laugh creeping into my voice, remembering how cringe that guy was. But then that laugh falls flat down to the ground, because of course people are probably saying the same about me.

'Remember that loser who couldn't even get through five minutes of being onstage? And he wants to be a proper comedian? LOL.'

'Does it make you feel better?' Dexter asks. 'Seeing that you're not bottom? There's only a point between you and the person above you. I told you your shit was good. Even just a few minutes of it.' He elbows me in the side, and I know I'm supposed to smile, thank him for the compliment, then make a toilet joke. But I can't help but think maybe it would have been better if I *was* last. There wouldn't be this seed of hope blooming in me. Hope is supposed to be a good thing, but somehow right now it's making me bubble with anxiety. There's hope within me of getting better, of getting above Nick Miller, who's just above me, and then above Sophie Hart, who's two points above him. There's a chance. But . . . there's also a chance that it won't happen. And I don't want to get my hopes up just to be crushed.

'Well?' Dexter prompts, oblivious to the tsunami inside my gut right now.

I force a smile at him. 'Nick Miller's going down,' I say with the confidence I need to fake for the rest of the night.

'That's more like it!' Dexter says, wrapping an arm around my neck and pulling me close to him. 'We got this, mate.'

He lets go of me before walking towards the main hall. I'm supposed to follow, but my eyes find themselves glued to the board. I look up to the top, knowing Dexter will be somewhere there, and a smile automatically comes to my face when I see that he's second. He really is smashing it. And he deserves to. I follow him to the table we had last week. Sitting down in the same seat brings a wave of déjà vu. I look around and the same people are here. Bridgeport is a small town, probably not a lot of comedy fans, so it's a safe bet that most of the crowd here are family and friends of the contestants. Dexter's dad begged to come, but he won't let him, says it would be too cringe to have him here. I can't imagine Baba wanting to know what this competition is about, let alone asking to come and watch. I guess I can't be too hard on my family, considering I'm the one who refuses to tell them about my passion, about taking part in this. But it's just . . . I know how it would go. They would disapprove big time. Well, firstly, they wouldn't even really understand it. Wanting to tell jokes for a living isn't something my parents could ever comprehend. They like to stay within the established rules of our culture, and me being obsessed with something as left field as this wouldn't make any sense to them. Which is why I haven't told them about it, and I won't.

I literally can't imagine these two sides of my life colliding.

I don't get why the other contestants even *want* their families and friends here. Why would you want to risk them seeing you get heckled?

God, what if the same thing happens again tonight? I'm already sensing the bad feelings inside me. If someone heckles me again, I think I will literally break down onstage. I can't take it any more.

'Going for a piss,' Dexter says, getting up off his chair. He says something else, but it's a bit garbled, as if he's jumped into a pool and is talking from underwater. Or maybe I'm the one who's drowning. I look around and I'm alone. Dexter's gone already, even though I swear he just finished his sentence. There are so many people in here now. Too many people. There's no space to breathe. Everyone is sucking out the oxygen from the room. The hall itself is closing in. I can feel the walls moving. They're getting closer, closer, closer. They're going to be on me any second, crushing me.

It's happening. It's happening again.

I can't just sit here. I can't sit here and wait.

The darkness is coming into the corners of my vision. The walls are closing in.

The pressure of the room is squeezing my chest.

I need out.

I NEED TO GET OUT OF HERE.

I manage to stumble out into the hallway. There's so many people and I'm sure they all think I'm a weirdo, and they'd be right. I *am* a weirdo. Why does this keep happening to me? Why am I so defective?

I run down the corridor, no longer caring what people think, just knowing I need to get back to that back room where I can be alone. The same room I ended up in when this happened last week.

I run for what feels like forever, even though this community centre is tiny. The sound of the people in the main hall disappears, and I can't tell if that's because I'm now so far away or because my hearing isn't working. Maybe I'm going deaf. Everything in my body is shutting down. Maybe this really is how I go.

My legs are jelly now. I barely manage to push my way into the back room. The door swings open and I stumble over my own feet.

I need it to stop. Why won't it stop?

I collapse on the floor. My jelly legs can't keep me up any more. There's nothing left inside me. Nothing. These bad feelings are taking over. I'm not strong enough.

I lean back against the wall, knees up, pressed against my chest. I push my face into my knees and wrap myself so tightly into a ball that it's painful. I deserve the pain. I'm stupid. Worthless.

The waves of panic wash over me again and again and again. This literally feels like it. The end. The end of Ibrahim Malik. And what do I leave behind?

Absolutely jack shit.

The waves continue to crash over me, colliding in my chest, caving it in. The blood is pounding pounding pounding in my ears, but somehow . . . over it all, I hear her voice.

'Hey, Ibrahim,' she says.

8

She's back.

She's real.

She's here, in this room with me. The same room she suddenly disappeared from last time.

Unless . . . Am I making her up? Has she been imaginary this whole time? Just existing in my head? Everything is still blurry, but I can see her standing there in front of me, towering over me as I'm curled up on the floor. She's wearing the same electric-blue headscarf and black polka-dot dress. And as my vision clears completely, I can see the look of concern on her face. The way her head's tilted, her eyes soft, her mouth in a slight frown as if she's worried I'm about to break completely.

'Deep breaths,' she says. Her voice travels to me as if through a tunnel, distorted. And by instinct I become aware of my breath. Sharp and shallow and definitely not bringing in enough oxygen. I'm going to die. I'm going to suffocate right here right now.

'C'mon, Ibrahim, focus,' she says, dropping down to the ground in front of me. Her voice is deeper this time. Authoritative. She crosses her legs and sits facing me about a metre away. 'Breathe in through your nose and out through your mouth. Like this.' She takes in a deep breath and then exhales, watching me the whole time. The next time she does it, I mirror her.

'Good, good,' she says chirpily. 'Try counting as you breathe.' She takes another deep breath, counting up to five on her fingers as she inhales, and then back down as she exhales. I find myself counting the numbers in my head alongside her, matching her breaths. We do this for God knows how long, but I'm so focused on following her instructions, on keeping my breath in time with hers, on counting as she drops her fingers that it takes me a while to notice that the bad feelings inside me have gone. My entire body loosens at the realisation, and I let myself relax. My arms let go of their death grip on my knees, my fingers white from where I've been clenching them. Relief floods my body. It's over. It's finally over.

And it's only now that I realise how intensely the strange girl is staring at me. She's smiling, but she's staring. Like, right at me. It freaks me the fuck out.

'Who are you?' I blurt. 'Why are you always in here?'

'My name's Sura,' she says with a smile that turns into a smirk. 'And I guess I just . . . like the decor.' She looks around the room – at the pale green walls covered in scuff marks, at the dirty window, at the carpet that's peeling up at the edges. Then she turns her gaze back on me. I want to ask her more questions, but the intensity of her stare is scaring me a bit.

'I should go,' I say, putting my palms on the floor. 'I've got to go do my set.' I push my hands against the rough carpet and try to get up. I flop back down almost immediately – my body is still so weak.

'Take it easy, Ibrahim,' she says, reaching a hand out as if to help me, or maybe to push me back down.

'I need to get back,' I say, making no effort to move again. I know there's no point.

'You need to learn how to deal with these panic attacks,' she says, ignoring me. 'They're just going to get worse.'

'Dexter's probably waiting for me,' I say, ignoring her right back. I look towards the door, willing him to come crashing in like he did last time. That was when Sura disappeared. I'm surprised he's not looking for me actually. I must have been in here for ages.

'Ibrahim?' Sura says. 'Don't you want my help?'

That gets me. I turn back to her, look her right in the eyes. 'How . . . how can you help?' I find myself asking.

A cheeky smile spreads across her face, replacing her intensity. 'That got your attention, huh?' she says.

'Can you make them stop?' I ask. 'Whatever . . . whatever this is . . . do you know what's causing it? How to make it stop?' A ray of hope blooms within me.

'Well, for starters, you need to acknowledge what *it* is. They're panic attacks, Ibrahim. You just had another panic attack.'

The shield that comes up every time that phrase is mentioned comes up within me. 'That's *not* what it is. I'm not –'

'I think, deep down, you know I'm telling the truth,' she says, a bit more softly. 'Acknowledging it will help, Ibrahim. Labelling it will help. Knowing more about what panic attacks are and how they work will help.'

I don't see how something as simple as giving something a name can help. Not with something as powerful as . . . whatever keeps happening to me.

'I've seen this happen to you twice now,' she says. 'And I'm betting it's happened a bunch more times, right?'

I don't give her the satisfaction of nodding.

'And each time I'm guessing it's been the same thing. The same feelings. And each time . . . they've stopped, eventually. Now, I could read you the classic list of symptoms if that would help you . . .'

'I'm not . . . this isn't . . .' I mutter, but with much less conviction.

'OK, first is a racing heartbeat. D'you have a racing heartbeat, Ibrahim?'

I do. But I can't tell her that.

'Shortness of breath? I mean, that was clear from our little breathing exercises,' Sura says. 'How about an overwhelming feeling of dread?'

I look up and meet her gaze. I can't tell from her tone whether she's making fun of me, but one look into her kind, caring eyes shows me she's not. She's . . . trying. She's trying to help. She . . . cares? I don't know why, but she seems to really care. And here I am being a dick.

But . . . I've never had an issue with my mental health. Never felt like hurting myself, never sat in a dark room crying because of how I feel.

But then . . . I think about what the doctor said the other day, about how panic attacks can happen to anyone. That it doesn't mean I'm crazy, or that I'm sick. Maybe it's because of all the stress, participating in this competition and shit. And stuff at home is stressful too.

That's all this is. Not because there's a problem in me. Just . . . how things are.

'Are you sweating?' Sura asks. 'Let me check your pits.' She leans across as if she's really about to touch me under my arm, but I swat her hand away.

'OK, OK, fine,' I say, resigned. 'It was . . . a panic attack. I have panic attacks.'

9

I expect her to make fun of me, or to gloat about the fact she made me say it out loud, that she made me accept it.

But she doesn't.

She's just looking on at me, legs crossed, hands in her lap, with a half-smile on her face. The word I'd use to describe her face is kind. Which is weird because *people* are kind, not faces, but it seems to fit. And then I start to think maybe . . . just maybe she can help me. She seems to know so much about what's happening to me. When I get these panic attacks, I always seem to find my way to her. So maybe she'll know what to do.

'So . . . how do I get them to stop happening?' I ask, tentatively, inwardly shivering at the idea that she might have the answers. That she might know how to fix me.

'Well, the best thing to do would be to find a therapist you can work with to explore your thoughts and emotions and figure out what's causing them in the first place.'

I give her a look. 'I don't need a therapist. I don't have any . . . thoughts and emotions I need to figure out.'

She gives me a look right back. 'There's always a cause,

Ibrahim. And unless you get to the root, then your panic attacks aren't going to go away.'

'I *don't* need a therapist,' I repeat, through gritted teeth. She offers me help and *this* is what she comes up with?

'Therapists can help everyone, Ibrahim. Having someone to talk to can –'

'If you're not going to give me something useful, I'm going to leave,' I say harshly. I uncross my legs and stand up, thanking my body for actually cooperating.

'Wait wait wait,' Sura says, also getting up off the floor. 'I can . . . I can give you some techniques to use. Just as . . . just as a coping mechanism.'

I can see she wants to help, and she's being nice. So I should be nice back. Or else she might disappear again. 'What kind of techniques?' I ask.

She smiles. Full-on grins at this. 'OK, so let's take this step by step. Think back to the other day, the first time we met. What caused that panic attack? Tell me about what happened. What was going through your head?'

'Well, I was onstage,' I say. 'Doing my stand-up set. I was feeling . . .' I pause. Both because I can't find the words to describe it, and because I'm still a bit wary of telling her. Of being open about what goes on in my head, about the worries that are lodged constantly there. Worries about my life, my family . . . everything. I can't tell her all this, can I? She'd think I was mental. Although I get the sense she already thinks that.

'You can trust me,' she says softly. 'What you say in here goes no further, I promise.'

'Are you trying to therapise me?' I ask.

She laughs. 'Something like that. If you want me to help you, you have to be open and honest. Otherwise there's no point.'

I nod and take a deep breath. 'I was . . . I was nervous. So nervous. About being onstage for the first time, about performing in front of all those people. I've always wanted to do comedy, but that was my first . . . proper step in making it happen. I'd been worrying about people's reactions the whole time, so when these guys at the back started heckling me –'

'Ooh!' Sura pipes up all squeaky and excited. I give her a confused look. 'Sorry, sorry! I didn't mean to be rude. I just . . . I thought of something. OK, so this is going to be . . . a bit weird, but don't freak out. I think this will really help you. Will help me teach you. OK?'

I stare at her, still confused, but she seems so excited about whatever this is that I just nod.

'OK, so . . . close your eyes,' Sura says.

My instinct is to make a joke about what she's going to do to me when I can't see, but I'm too curious about how she can help, so I just follow her instructions.

'Think back to that night. Being onstage, everyone watching you.'

I can picture it so vividly in my mind. The way the lights were dim, but bright enough to show me the wide mocking mouths of the hecklers, the way the room felt so big, too big to run out of, but at the same time as if it was closing in on me.

'Now open your eyes,' Sura basically whispers – there's still excitement laced in her voice.

When I open my eyes, I'm not in the small back room with the rough green carpet any more. I'm back in the main hall. Standing at the back of the hall watching . . . watching myself onstage?!

What the fuck?!

10

This is the weirdest thing ever. Sura and I stand next to each other, behind all the tables, near the cork noticeboard at the back with a giant 'MISSING' poster for a cat that looks possessed. And on the stage on the opposite side of the room is . . . can I call it me? *I'm* me, but then who's that . . . ? How!?

'What the fuck is happening?!' I ask, turning to Sura. 'How can I be here . . . and there? What . . . ?!' It's almost cartoonish, the way my head flicks back and forth between the stage and Sura like someone watching a game of table tennis. I'm waiting for things to click in my head, for it to suddenly make sense, but I just end up getting dizzy from moving my head so much.

'I can't fully explain it,' Sura says. 'Not in a way that makes sense. But think of it like reliving a memory, except you get to see it from different angles. Don't worry – no one can see or hear us.'

'But . . . how?' I ask, exasperated. 'How can this be real?'

'Who says it's real?' She wiggles her eyebrows at me. She must notice my expression cos her smile drops a little. She rolls her eyes playfully. 'It's just . . . Let's call it magic. Will that make it easier for you?'

'I don't believe in magic,' I reply. 'Unless you're talking about black magic. My mum always says to stay away from that.'

'Mine too! It's an Asian mum thing, right?' She smiles. 'But this is a good type of magic. Not black. Also, now that I think about it, that's quite racist, right? Calling the bad kind of magic *black*.' She laughs a little to herself. 'Anyway, I promise this'll be good. It'll help, and that's what you want, right?'

'Am I . . . am I dreaming or something?' I say quietly. 'This must be a dream, yeah?'

She reaches over and pinches my arm. I flinch and cry out in pain.

'Believe it's real now?' she asks.

'But *how*?' I ask desperately. 'I just –'

'Shhh, shh,' she says, urgently tapping my arm. 'It's about to get interesting.' She twists me so we're facing a table where two girls are sitting. They look like uni students, each with a half-empty bottle of some blue liquid in front of them. I expect them to look up any second, see us standing there and ask us what the fuck we're doing, spying on them. My heartrate spikes again.

'So you were saying how you were scared people weren't going to like your material, right? You were worried that people would boo you off the stage?'

'Yeah,' I say. 'And that's exactly what happened.'

'Or did it?' she says theatrically. She turns to me and she's got the biggest grin with wide eyes. Honestly, she looks disturbing.

I'm about to say something when a loud wave of laughter begins around the room. I glance up at myself onstage, thinking this must be it – this must be the moment it all fell apart. But

I look fine onstage. There's a smile on my face, I'm standing tall. Although, dear God, my shirt is so creased. How did I not notice that before I left the house?

The crowd . . . they're not laughing at *me*. They're laughing at my joke.

I look around and there are people with genuine-looking smiles on their faces. The laughter lasts way longer than the polite little chuckle I was expecting.

I feel Sura's fingers digging into my upper arm, and turn to her. She gestures with her head towards the girls in front of us.

'He's real good, innit?' the blonde one says to her friend.

The black-haired girl looks to the me onstage. She's laughing, all relaxed and enjoying herself. '*So* funny,' she agrees.

They think I'm funny? I feel a smile flicker on my own face. Someone actually thinks my set is good. All those hours practising were worth it.

'See?' Sura hisses next to me. 'These girls love your set. Does hearing that make you feel better?'

I think about it for a second before my instinctive reaction kicks in. 'They're . . . they're just being nice,' I say. 'They probably don't mean it.'

'They don't think anyone else is listening – why would they say something they don't mean?' Sura asks.

I shrug. 'Just . . . They're being nice. Maybe they pity me, I dunno.' This conversation is starting to make me uncomfortable now. Why can't she see that they don't mean it? That they *can't* mean it.

'You wanted techniques to help with the panic attacks and negative thoughts, right?' she asks.

I shrug and nod a little. Panic attacks, yes, but negative thoughts? I guess my thoughts are negative mostly. I hadn't realised.

'So a technique that really helps me with negative thoughts is to try and back them up with facts. Thoughts are naturally biased and subjective. But facts are irrefutable. So, let's try it now. You say these girls don't mean what they're saying. That they don't really believe you're good at comedy. Try and back that thought up with facts.'

I think about it for a few seconds. 'They're . . . They can see that I'm . . . struggling,' I say. 'They're just being nice.'

'And what is the evidence for that?' Sura asks, patiently. 'Facts need evidence. This is all your perception. There's no way of knowing. Also . . . it doesn't make sense. If they were *just* being nice, they'd do it to your face.' She pauses before continuing. 'So, can you think of any actual *facts*?'

I try. I try and come up with actual hard facts, try and find some evidence, because I *know* I'm right, but . . . nothing comes.

'Thought not,' Sura says after a few seconds. I expect her to be smug, but she sounds gentle and sincere. 'There are, however, *many* facts to support the opposite thought. And that's the way this technique works. First you try and back up your thought, and then you try and find facts to negate that thought. So for one, the facts are that these people are strangers, right? You've never seen them before?'

I nod, reluctantly, knowing that she's going to prove me wrong, and that that'll feel all weird.

'So they have nothing to gain from stroking your ego. From "just being nice". Fact two, you're literally in a stand-up competition. You're here to make people laugh, for them to think you're funny. So you're successful in that respect. You heard the laughter all through the audience, not just from this table. I saw the way your face transformed hearing that, hearing them cheering for you, for your talent. That's what you wanted. That's what you deserve, Ibrahim. You have to just learn to train your brain like this. To not accept the negative thoughts it comes up with. You need to –'

She's cut off by a deep voice a few tables over yelling, 'You suck! Get off the stage and go get your eyes fixed, four-eyes!'

My head whips round to the table with the group of five guys, all clearly drunk. One of them spits out his drink all over the table cos he's laughing so hard. I turn from them to the me onstage, because I know what's about to happen.

I can literally see my face freeze, my rhythm interrupted. I can see the effect the words have on me, the way my body tenses and my eyes flick back and forth, the panic rising inside me. My own heart now, in the present, speeds up just watching Past Me. It feels like it might happen all over again, that I might have another panic attack right here right now in this weird dream memoryscape. But then I feel fingers digging into my arm again. Sura.

'Look at them,' she commands.

I turn back to the table of drunk guys, but looking at them reminds me exactly how shit I felt, all because of that one comment. And here they are, laughing it up.

'Did you hear him?' Sura asks. 'Fact number one: he didn't heckle you on your set, or your material. Fact number two: he obviously wasn't thinking much about his insult, considering he relied on a super-basic cliché. Third fact: they're all drunk. They came here to do exactly this. They get a kick out of knocking people down. They've been heckling everyone who's been up onstage all night.'

'No, they haven't,' I say, still unable to take my eyes off them. 'They didn't heckle Dexter.'

'Uh, yes, they did,' Sura says. 'Less glasses-based mockery, of course, but they still made fun of him.'

'What?!' I turn my head to her. 'That's not true. I was there. I was watching. No one said anything bad about Dexter. His stuff is too good.'

'You were so preoccupied with your own thoughts and worries that you weren't paying attention. I promise you they did the exact same thing to Dexter, and to all the other contestants.'

I'm about to tell her she's lying again, that she's just saying it to make me feel better, but my phone chirps, loud and foreign in among the weird scene we're in right now. I pull my phone out of my jeans pocket and see a text from Dexter.

Where u gone? Ima kill u if uve done a runner

He sounds pissed off. He must think I've ditched him. How long have I even been gone?

When I look up again, I'm no longer in the main hall. Sura and I are back in that small room with the stacks of chairs in the corner.

'What the fuck?' I say, looking around. 'How the hell did that happen?'

'We already had this conversation,' Sura says. 'Magic, remember?'

My phone starts ringing before I have a chance to ask any more questions. It's Dexter.

'I have to go,' I say quickly. The reality of the situation is starting to set in now. Somehow I've moved through time and space and I'm still not entirely sure if this girl is a hundred per cent real. Though her grip on my arm certainly is.

'One last thing,' she says.

'Dexter's waiting,' I tell her, looking towards the door.

'Just . . . promise me you'll try something,' she pleads. 'Whenever you have an overwhelming negative thought, try to think of three facts to back it up, and then three facts to contradict it. Just try it. It will help. Promise me you'll try?'

My phone keeps ringing, and I can hear footsteps outside now. Dexter's probably come looking for me. I give Sura a quick nod before opening the door and walking out.

11

Dexter has a real go at me for running off. I tell him I'll buy him a Snickers bar to apologise and he immediately forgives me. We go back into the main hall and sit at a table near the front but off to the side. Our normal table. Everyone here seems to be in the same seats as last time. Basically like we're in school. I recognise some of the faces, which helps calm my nerves a teeny bit. One of the other competitors – the guy who made the boring fish jokes – even smiles at me. It's a nice atmosphere. It really feels like I could fit in here. That these could be my people.

'So my therapist suggested I give my anxiety a name, and I chose the name Mildred,' the woman onstage, Sophie Hart, says. 'Because that's such an ugly name, which is so apt for anxiety. Oh, sorry to any Mildreds out there, but I'm sure you've had worse.' She's doing great. Tonight's a bit different in the way it's set up. Each contestant is given a broad category, and we have to use that as a prompt for our set. Improv has always been a bit scary to me – the idea of not being able to prepare freaks me out a little. Well, a lot, actually. But Dexter taught me a workaround when we found out about this a few days ago.

The trick, he says, is to make it into a planned set. To come up with a bunch of jokes and anecdotes that can be twisted to fit any theme or topic that comes up. I don't know how well it'll work in practice, but it's made me feel a little less terrified. It seems a bit more manageable. It should be fine . . . unless . . .

I look around the room again. Yep, all the same people are here. Including . . .

'Oh, shit,' I end up saying out loud.

Dexter follows my gaze, looking at the group of very drunk lads in their football shirts at the table near the bar.

'Oh, God, those fuckers are back?' Dexter says. It makes me feel a bit better to see that he remembers them, that he knows they're pricks, that Dexter is as bothered by them as I am. At least this isn't just me being a pussy. 'Let's hope they get chucked out again before either of us has to go up.'

'Wait, they got chucked out?' I ask. I turn back to see if he's lying, making this up just to make me feel better, but his face looks normal. In fact, he looks a bit angry.

'Yeah,' Dexter says, turning back to watch Sophie again. 'They were being dicks, calling out stuff at everyone, taking the piss. I think some people complained about them, and the manager kicked them out. Thank fuck.'

'They heckled other people?' I ask. 'I was . . . I watched other people's sets. I watched *your* set. They didn't have a go at anyone else. It was . . . it was just me, no?'

Dexter looks at me, eyebrow raised. 'You didn't hear them tell me to kill myself and join my mum?'

'What?!' I ask, shocked. 'No way. I was . . . I was there. I was listening . . . I would have heard . . .'

I think back to what Sura said, that I was so preoccupied with my own worries that I wasn't paying full attention. She was right – I'm an awful friend. Here I've been worrying only about myself, thinking that they singled me out, when they attacked my best friend too. The friend who spent ages calming me down that night, who's spent hours and hours encouraging me to do this, helping me prepare for tonight and the competition as a whole.

'It almost threw me,' Dexter says. 'But then I thought the best thing to do was to ignore them, y'know? It's why I was so worried about the scores this week. Those pricks got into my head.'

My brain is almost exploding now. This can't be right. Dexter is . . . He's so good at this. He's normally so calm, so collected. He's so quick on his feet and never gets rattled by things other people say. There was a whole term where everyone kept making jokes about him actually having killed his mum (because of the TV serial killer namesake he has), and I know it really got to him, but he always had the best comebacks – a different one each time. Like a real pro. But now he's saying those drunken idiots got to him too? I literally can't believe it.

A loud wave of laughter runs through the entire room, and my attention goes back to the stage, where Sophie is standing there, grinning out at the crowd, basking in the approval. She paces a little as she waits for the laughter and clapping to die down.

'Everyone has a story of when they "knew",' Sophie continues. 'And for me, it was during a conversation with a friend. I opened up about the fact that at any given time I have about twenty tabs open in my brain, right? I'm worrying about whether my cat has eaten enough, whether he hates me, I'm thinking about my sick grandma, and that I haven't picked up vitamins for her in a while. I'm even worrying about the old lady who lives next door, who I haven't seen in a week. It's just . . . Mildred is non-stop in my head. And so I tell this to my friend, right? And I say, "You know what I mean, right?" Because I legit thought everyone did. And her response? "Um, not really. Most of the time all I'm thinking about is what I'm having for dinner."'

The crowd laughs, but I'm gripped, watching her. Everything she's saying . . . fits me perfectly. Fits my experiences perfectly. Could it be . . . ?

Sophie's talking about her anxiety . . . so openly. As if she's . . . proud? As if she wants people to know, rather than hiding it. And the weird thing is, no one is judging her. No one's thinking it's weird. They're . . . smiling. Maybe they relate too? How many people here are like that? I wonder if there's anyone else in here looking up to the stage, listening to her and inwardly nodding. I look over to Dexter, and he's watching her with a smile on his face. No one else seems to be having the same revelation as me.

'SHOW US YOUR TITS!' a deep voice calls out. Everyone's heads turn towards the noise, which is of course coming from the table of drunk idiots. They all laugh and pat the guy who shouted on the back. Ugh.

'Just hold a mirror up to you and your mates,' Sophie replies calmly. 'Huge set of tits right there.' Another wave of laughter goes around the audience as the guys at the table scowl. People start clapping for Sophie as she finishes her set, but all I can do is watch the drunk guys at the table. Watch as the manager comes over to their table, says some words I can't hear over the applause. The guys start waving their arms and protesting. It looks like there's going to be a fight. But then another man comes over, stands next to the manager. This man is ripped as hell, and the drunk boys immediately quieten down and start downing their drinks. A few seconds later they're picking up their jackets and leaving.

Relief floods my body. They're going. They won't be here for my set. I won't have to look at them, wondering when they'll burst out with the insults, won't have to be on edge, just waiting for them to get in my head. This means I might actually have a chance to get some decent points.

When I turn back to face the stage, Sophie has gone. The audience is quiet again. There's a woman on the stage I recognise as one of the judges. She's got some paper in her hand, and she glances directly at me. My heart spikes a little, but then she smiles, and it gets a bit better.

'Please welcome up Ibrahim *Malik*,' she says, emphasising my surname and pronouncing it properly to make up for last time. It makes me smile a little.

'Break a leg,' Dexter says to me as I get up. 'No, really. Break a leg. It'd be hilarious.'

The audience is clapping for me, and my body is slowly turning to jelly. But the fact those guys have left makes me feel so much better. So much more confident. I can do this. I can. I think back to what Sura said. I just have to get through this set, and then the next. One step at a time.

God, who even am I? Where's all the panic and anxiety?

70

Before I know it, I'm onstage, standing under the lights, with everyone looking up at me. And it's too late to get scared now. I just have to fake it till I make it. Another one of Dexter's tips. I look down at him, and he's hooting for me. Giant grin on his face. It makes me smile. Makes me confident.

I take a deep breath, just like Sura showed me – in through the nose, out through the mouth. I take the mic in my hand and look out to the crowd. My eyes land on the two women at the back, the ones who thought I was funny last time. The blonde woman is smiling.

I can do this.

It's going to be OK.

'Hey, everyone, I'm Ibrahim,' I say. I look to my right, to the judge standing there with her clipboard. 'I'm really hoping my topic for the night is gonna be "experiences as a white woman" cos I think that might be my specialist subject.'

The crowd chuckles lightly, which lifts me up a little. The judge smiles and looks down at her paper.

I got this.

12

The high from round two of the stand-up competition lasts for days. I did well. I know I did. I was thrown a little by getting politics as my topic, but Dexter's advice about preparing then tweaking worked. And more than that, I found myself actually coming up with new jokes on the spot. I thought I'd hate the pressure of improv, that the bad thoughts and the anxiety would creep in again, but weirdly . . . I felt good up there. Like I belonged. The applause on my way down the steps was like everyone welcoming me into a group I've been dying to get into my whole life. It feels like I've found my people. I've found my place. Even if the judges don't give me enough points to rise up in the ranks, it's fine because I'm feeling better. I'm feeling good. It's the first time in a long time I've had confidence in myself.

And the good mood is most welcome today, since I'm at a family gathering. One of my cousins has rented out a huge hall, got a bunch of caterers, custom-made cakes and desserts, decorations and shit, just to celebrate their kid's first birthday. It's insanely extravagant, but actually not surprising. People do this crap all the time. And invite hundreds of people. As if the baby is ever going to remember this.

The baby may not appreciate any of it, but I personally really appreciate the dessert table. There's so many different things here – cakes and biscuits and even individual cheesecakes. Mariyam had one of everything, then went running off on a sugar high. This venue has a water fountain at the front. A real kid magnet. We came here for a wedding last year and Mariyam wouldn't shut up about it for weeks after. I remember I was so scared that she'd drown or something that I spent most of my time following her around, watching her from the balcony on the third floor, carrying samosas in my pocket for when she'd come up to me complaining that she was hungry. I couldn't find her at one point and had to go asking random people if they'd seen her. I had to talk to actual strangers, describing her to make sure she hadn't been kidnapped or something. I remember a girl on the balcony ended up finding her for me, and – surprise, surprise – Mariyam was back at the fountain. I should have guessed! I thanked the girl by giving her a squashed samosa that Mariyam had been making me save. I thought I was being nice, but the girl started crying and ran away. I cringed about that for days afterwards.

Everything ended up fine with Mariyam though, so this time I leave her to her water-fountain shenanigans, instead sitting at a table with my family. Ma and Baba are having a whale of a time, catching up with relatives they haven't seen in a while, gossiping away. We live so far away from most of our family – the only time they get to see everyone properly is at weddings, or I guess at ridiculously extravagant first-birthday parties. They're currently sat with Auntie Kameela, the biggest gossip ever. Hamza and I lounge on the other side of the table, both on our phones, both bored out of our minds.

'Have you seen this one?' Hamza asks. He tilts his phone so I can see the screen. A video plays of a cat being scared by a cucumber and I snort-laugh.

'Six–three to me,' he says, taking the phone back. This is a game we play at family gatherings: try and make each other laugh.

'Not my fault you're a joyless robot,' I say, breaking open a filled biscuit embossed with the birthday baby's name. I take the side without cream and give the other half to Hamza, before scrolling down TikTok looking for a video to beat him.

After a minute I feel someone tugging on my shirt and turn to find Mariyam standing there, all red-faced. Panic strikes my heart. There's something wrong. I can tell by the colour of her face, the pain in her expression.

'Inhaler,' she wheezes.

Mariyam's struggled with asthma since she was little, though she hasn't had an attack for almost two years now.

Hamza and I share a panicked look. 'Ma!' I call quickly, desperately.

She looks over, annoyed at me for breaking up her chat. Then notices Mariyam. Her eyes widen and she jumps up out of her chair and rushes over.

'What's wrong?' she asks, looking Mariyam in the face. She bends over and puts her hands on Mariyam's shoulders.

'She needs her inhaler – do you have it?' I ask. My heart's thump-thump-thumping away. Mariyam's struggling to breathe.

I can hear the rasp. She needs that inhaler *now* and Ma's just standing there staring at her. Why isn't she moving? WHY?

'Inhaler?' she asks, confused. As if she's completely forgotten Mariyam has asthma. 'I haven't . . . I didn't bring it. She doesn't use an inhaler any more, does she?'

Ma looks right at me, as if I have all the answers. I guess she knows I'm supposed to. I'm the one who pays attention at Mariyam's appointments. Ma just comes cos they need an adult there. I'm the one who listens to what the doctors say about how to manage her condition. I'm supposed to know. I should have brought her inhaler with me, just in case. This is all my fault.

There's tingling in my fingers, pressure in my chest.

Oh no.

No no no no.

Not here. Not now.

I can't have a panic attack in front of all these people. In front of my parents! No no NO!

'Oh!' I hear Ma's voice, distorted through my blocked ears. She's moved further away now, back towards her seat. Mariyam's there with her too. When did they move?! 'Look, your auntie Kameela has one for Idrees!' Ma says.

I watch through slightly blurry eyes as Auntie Kameela hands Ma a blue inhaler – one that does look exactly like Mariyam's. Ma helps Mariyam take a big puff.

I need to leave. I can't be here when the panic attack fully hits.

If Auntie Kameela hadn't had that inhaler today, what would have happened? We'd have had to call an ambulance, taken her to hospital. People die from asthma attacks, don't they? And it would have been my fault. I should have been on top of it.

The panic's rising again. I need to stop it.

What would Sura say?

Think of three facts to back up your thought, and three facts against it.

I can do this. I can, I can, I can.

OK. Three facts to back up the idea that this is all my fault.

Fact one: I've been to every one of Mariyam's appointments. I know the signs, I know how bad it can get. I should be prepared for everything.

That's not a fact! I can practically hear Sura's voice in my head.

I think. I think and I think and I think. But . . . that's all I can come up with. No actual facts.

I try the other way round. Three facts to back up the idea that this *isn't* my fault.

Fact one: Mariyam hasn't had an asthma attack or needed her inhaler for over a year. No one could have anticipated this. We couldn't have known. She runs around a lot at home, and at school. She's always been fine with that.

Fact two: back when Mariyam *did* need her inhaler regularly, she was always weirdly grown-up about it. She could recite exactly what the medicine did to her body, and knew how to identify a bad asthma day. She's always been pretty much in charge of her own health, and I guess I just expected that to carry on.

Fact three: my parents should have thought about this. How hard is it to always carry an inhaler, just in case? Ma always has a handbag. An inhaler is tiny. This is their job as parents. Auntie Kameela had hers for her son ready in an instant. Ma should be like this.

OK, so that last one isn't a fact, but two is better than nothing. And it . . . it's actually helped a bit. I remind myself no one could have prepared for something this unexpected. And Mariyam seems . . . She seems OK now. She's smiling, probably just loving the attention, and the colour on her face appears to have gone back to normal. I should just be grateful that everything worked out.

It's OK.

Everything is OK.

I take another deep breath.

It worked. Sura's technique worked.

Ma stops Mariyam from running back out to the fountain, makes her sit next to Hamza. They begin watching an episode of *Creature Clinic* (some animal show Mariyam loves) together. The panic inside me begins to ebb away. And from now on I'll always remember to make sure someone has Mariyam's inhaler when we're out. I go over to the dessert table and pick up a chocolate frosted cupcake, again personalised with a photo of the baby's face (which I take off and leave on the table because biting into a cupcake that has creepy baby eyes staring up at you makes me feel a bit like a cannibal).

As I bite into the cupcake, I start thinking about Sura. I can't help but wonder if she's a real person. I mean, she can do some kind of magic so I guess she's not real at all, and probably just a figment of my imagination. A hallucination? A dream that feels very close to real life when I'm having a panic attack? But I read this thing once that said all the people you see in your dreams have the face of someone you've seen in real life. So where have I seen Sura before? She seems weirdly familiar. Again, maybe that's because I invented her in my head. Or maybe . . . maybe she's real and a relative. She's Bengali, so I'm sure we're linked *somehow*.

I look at the faces of the women and girls all around the room as I eat my baby-face-less cupcake. I try and do it casually so no one thinks I'm perving. I scan faces, looking for anyone that looks like her. I stop mid-bite when I see her trademark electric-blue headscarf. There's a girl – about her height, standing with her back to me, a bit further up. Could it be her? Would it be weird if I went up to her? Would she even know who I was? What if she doesn't recognise me and I tell her about everything and it sounds like I dream about this random stranger? That's a sure way to get labelled a pervert.

But . . . I have to, right? I mean, if it *is* her, I need to know. I need to talk to her, to understand what the hell is happening between us.

I drop the half-eaten cupcake onto the table and wipe my mouth – don't want to be going up to her with chocolate all over my face. God, what am I going to say to her? How would I introduce myself? Do I even need to? Maybe she'll recognise me straight away and say one of her cheesy phrases like, 'I've been expecting you.'

I start walking over, feeling sweat begin to bead on my forehead, drip down my back. My heart's thudding again, but this time with nervousness rather than sheer panic. I just need to go up to her, tap her on the shoulder, and see if her eyes light up with recognition when she sees me.

I'm a few metres away from her when she stops looking down at her phone. She looks up, and turns around, so she's facing me. As if she knew I was coming.

'Hey, Ibrahim.'

'Oh, hey, Sabrina,' I say to my cousin.

We stand and chat for a while. Sabrina's getting married soon, and so of course can't shut up about it, even though I very clearly am not the type to care about weddings. I just nod every now and then as she speaks.

I'm so disappointed it wasn't Sura. But just because she's not here doesn't mean she's not real, right? She *must* be real. She can't just be someone I imagined. I may be coming to terms with the idea of having panic attacks, and possibly some mental health issues, but there's no way I'm crazy enough to have created an entire person in my head.

Sabrina finally walks off in search of someone more interested in the colour scheme for her mehndi, and I grab myself another cupcake and sit down at an empty table, not ready to go back to my family yet. I get out my phone and pull up Instagram. I type Sura's name in the search box. But I don't know her last name. She never told me it. When I type in just 'Sura', all I get are pictures of someone from a baking show that everyone loves. I try Facebook instead, just in case she's old school. And there are lots of Suras there. But none of them are my Sura. None of them have that same kind face, those caring eyes.

I try Google next. I need to prove she exists. If she's not real, then none of this is real. The advice she's given me, the way she's made me feel, the way she's changed me. How can any of that be real if *she's* not real? Real people can . . . take me into memories, right? That's totally a human thing.

Google just comes back with more photos of the cake lady, now walking a cat on a lead.

Gah! I give up.

I bite into another chocolate frosted cupcake, this time tearing the baby's face in half.

13

The sun is shining super hard today. Sun automatically puts me in a good mood. Add to that the fact that it's an INSET day, and you've got all the ingredients to make a happy Ibrahim. Baba, Hamza and I are at Friday Jummah prayers at the community centre. It's weird to see people kneeling down to pray in the same place where just the other day I sat and cheered for Dexter as he smashed another set. Weird to see the imam standing in the exact spot I stood and felt for the first time in my life like I could actually be a comedian.

It's one of those days where it feels like everything is in place. There's no panic, no anxiety. No sadness, no worry. Alhamdulillah, I'm just feeling pretty good. It's apt that we're doing our prayers, because I feel like I need to give my thanks to Allah. For things slowly becoming better. It's been over a week since I last had a panic attack. It doesn't feel weird saying that any more, which is miraculous in itself. I know now it's not something I'm responsible for, and it's not something to feel ashamed about. I still wouldn't openly talk about it though. I guess I won't have to, now that they've stopped. I genuinely think I've kicked it for good. I've not even had to use Sura's facts technique, or her breathing thing. I just have to avoid stress – that seems to be my trigger. Just got to make sure that I can identify the bad thoughts and stop them before they become too much.

I guess I've got Sura to thank for this. She's basically my guardian angel. As the imam finishes up, I say a little prayer for her. She deserves all the good. I wonder if I can slip off to the back room and see if she's in there. It would be nice to see her at a time I'm not feeling like I'm about to die. I watch as Baba goes over to talk to the imam, shake hands with some of the other people. He takes forever to leave after Jummah. Hamza and I always get bored waiting around.

But then . . . a small twinge in my chest. And a weird feeling starts radiating around my heart. I look over at Hamza leaning against the wall, on his phone. But I can't focus on him. My vision is starting to blur.

Oh no.

My heart is pounding, the sounds around me distorting.

It's happening again.

No way.

Why? Why is this happening?

I was . . . fine . . . I wasn't thinking anything bad. There was . . . nothing.

My legs are weak, and I have the urge to just drop to the ground.

WHY IS THIS HAPPENING?

Every other time there's been a cause, a trigger. But today I was happy! For the first time in a long time, I was feeling good. That's the opposite of a panic attack.

Sura lied. She promised me it would go away, that this would stop happening if I fought back against my bad thoughts, if I managed the stress, stopped the panic. Deep breaths and logical thinking. It was supposed to fix everything. WHY HASN'T THIS FIXED ANYTHING?

I need Sura. I need to go find her. Not just for her help, but I want to shout at her. If this can happen when I'm feeling OK, when I'm feeling good . . . then there's no way to predict it. How am I supposed to stop them if I don't know what causes them?

Sura promised her techniques would help, but I'm doing the breathing, I'm doing her counting thing, standing here in the middle of the main hall, sweating, about to collapse. But it's not working.

I need her.

I turn and run, almost stumbling because of the weakness in all my limbs. People are going to think I'm crazy. I know that. But I don't know what else to do.

I reach the door to the back room she's been in every time. There's such a heaviness in my chest now that it feels like I'll suffocate soon. I'll suffocate unless she tells me how to stop the panic attack. Tells me why this is happening in the first place.

I push the door open, expecting her to be standing there in her blue scarf and polka-dot dress. Expecting her to greet me with her 'Hey, Ibrahim' that I'll barely hear over the pounding in my ears.

But she's not there.

Instead, I'm met by a group of women, who all turn to look at me, shocked at my bursting in. A few women at the back are kneeling on their prayer mats, mid-namaz.

Oh shit. I forgot they do the women's prayers in here. I look around the room quickly. She must be here. She's always here. She's always here when I need her. WHY ISN'T SHE HERE?

'Are you OK?' one of the women asks. Her voice is distorted though, coming at me through waves and waves of panic.

'I . . . I'm sorry,' I manage to get out. I quickly back out of the room and close the door. I want so badly to just lean against a wall and drop to the ground. To curl up into a ball until this attack passes. But without Sura here, *how* do I get over it?

My breaths start coming faster and faster. Then I hear Sura's voice in my head, telling me to take deep breaths.

'In through your nose, out through your mouth.'

I close my eyes and picture her doing it in front of me. I make my breaths match hers, shakily, slowly, calmly.

'What are you doing?' I hear a voice say.

I jolt, eyes opening, body straightening. It's Hamza. He's looking at me all weird. Or maybe that's just because of my blurred vision.

I can't let him see me like this. I have to act normal. I have to *be* normal.

'Nothing,' I say. It doesn't come out as shaky as I thought it would.

I don't know what I look like right now, but all I can do is hope Hamza doesn't ask me what's wrong, ask me what's happening. If he tries to talk about it, I think I will just collapse onto the dirty carpet right here, right now. I can't let him know the truth. He'd think I was crazy. He probably already does.

'What's wr—' he starts.

'Nothing!' I repeat, shouting this time. Black spots appear in my vision.

'But wh—'

'Just stop, OK? Stop . . . just leave me alone.'

'Whatever, weirdo,' he says gruffly after a little pause. 'Baba's waiting for you to walk home. Hurry up.'

He turns and starts walking away, but I hear those words repeating in my head over and over.

Whatever, weirdo.

Baba's waiting. I need to go. Can I go when I'm like this? I still feel all wobbly, like my legs won't hold me up. But I have no choice. I can hear the women in the room approaching the door too.

I push back against the wall, taking those deep breaths, telling myself I can do this. I can pretend to be normal. I can totally walk home while having a panic attack. If I collapse on the way, I can blame it on the heat.

I start walking down the corridor. Like the weirdo I am.

14

I always like hanging out at Dexter's house. There are no shouting children, or demanding mothers, and no lingering smell of curry. There's no chance that I'll be called upon to fix something, or call someone, or drop what I'm doing at a moment's notice. I feel like I can be fully myself here.

It's nice.

Well, it *was* nice, before our revision session was interrupted by an email from the organisers of the stand-up competition.

'We have to work in GROUPS?' I exclaim, my heart already pounding.

I look over to Dexter, but he's still reading the email from his laptop screen. '*In random groups of three, you'll be given a situation to improvise,*' he reads out loud. His voice is calm. He's not bothered. And why would he be? He's always so cool and confident. But I'm freaking out hard. I have to work with *strangers*. It's hard enough doing this alone, with tons of practice and a memorised set, but throw in strangers, and being put on the spot, and you've got a recipe for disaster. I don't know if it's even *possible* to prepare for this. You can't predict anything when there are other people in the mix.

'God, what if we get put with the fish guy?' I groan.

Dexter laughs. 'At least you'd get good marks cos he'd be a train wreck.'

'The point of it is to riff off each other though, right? How the hell do you riff off someone who thinks reading out a list of weird fish names is funny?'

Dexter laughs again. 'I mean, watching it *was* quite funny, you have to admit,' he says. 'Not for the reasons he thought, but still.'

'How are you not freaking out?' I ask. 'We only ever practise solo stuff. How the hell can we even prepare for this?'

He shrugs lazily. 'As much as you can practise any improv. Just try shit out, see how it goes and roll with whatever seems to be working. At least there's two of us. The others probably don't have comic geniuses as best friends.'

'Yeah, you are pretty lucky,' I tease, feeling the shock and anger fading away with Dexter's reassurances.

He elbows me in the side. 'Um, excuse me? Who's number two in the rankings, again?'

This is the thing about our friendship. We can make jokes like this. We both want the best for each other. Dexter knows I'd never resent him for beating me. And if it were the other way round (which it never would be), I know he would be the same with me.

'You're number two all right,' I say.

'Booooo!' Dexter jeers. 'Be better onstage, man.'

'Ugh, I suck at improv. I'm not good on the spot.'

'Nah, but you are good at *getting* spots.' He pokes the painful spot on my chin and I whack his hand away with an 'Oi!'

'And anyway, you were great last week. That was improv.'

'What's going on in here then?' Dexter's dad says, coming into the living room where we've got books strewn over the table and floor. He's carrying a tray of two glasses of squash and a bowl of crisps. It's literally like one of those American soaps, where the family is so loving and . . . *normal*. That's what it's like being over here with Dexter and his dad. Like being in a soap. And just like in soaps, Dexter takes the role of grumpy teenager. He groans a little as his dad approaches.

'Just doing some revision,' I say to Mr Murgen, because I know Dexter won't say anything. I move some of our books from the table so that he can put the tray down. Again, because I know Dexter won't do anything. This is one thing that bugs me about Dexter. He's got such an amazing dad. Such a nice home life. Sure, his dad works a lot, but when he is around, he's always so attentive. He always asks Dexter and me about stuff, about school, even about how the comedy competition is going. He's over-the-top supportive of Dexter's dream to get into stand-up. Can you believe that? He takes him to comedy shows all the time. I can't even imagine *talking* to my dad about this. I'd have to explain what comedy is, why people pay to go and watch people making jokes. He'd never understand it. Mr Murgen does though. I've always secretly wished he was my dad. Even now, as he smiles at me as he puts the dishes on the table, I'm hit by how this is what it's like for everyone else. To have parents who ask what you're up to, in a way that means they're interested, and not because they want to know if it's important enough not to interrupt (it's never important enough not to interrupt).

But Dexter. Dexter doesn't appreciate that one bit. He

doesn't even look up once, even though his dad's obviously hovering, trying to get something out of him.

'How are you feeling about the next stage of the competition then, Ibrahim?' Mr Murgen asks.

I go to respond, but Dexter jumps in first. 'Oh God, please don't,' he groans. He finally looks up at his dad. 'We're trying to revise here. Can you get out?'

I cringe inwardly, and there's a flare of anger too. His dad is just being nice, and Dexter's being a prick back. Maybe we should swap lives for a while, see how he likes living in my family, and let me have a break, let me live in this happy, loving household where I could actually be a normal teenager and not just a third parent.

'Ib, can you grab my charger? It's in that cupboard over there,' Dexter says, once again completely ignoring his dad, who's just standing there, holding the empty plastic tray now.

It's so awkward, being in the middle of this moment, so I'm almost grateful for Dexter's request. Even though I want to make a dig about him being a lazy shit, I don't. I just get up and go over to the cabinets by the TV. As I open the door of the cupboard Dexter pointed at, something falls out, landing with a clatter on the wooden floor.

'Sorry!' I say, picking up the picture frame. I turn it over and see it's a photo of Dexter's mum. There's a big crack running through the middle of it.

'Oh my God, I'm so sorry,' I repeat, now realising that I've just broken a photo of his dead mother. I look at Dexter's dad, expecting him to be raging, but he's still got that smile on his face. His usual, easy, outgoing face.

'No worries,' he says, coming over and taking the frame from my hands. He doesn't even look at it, just shoves it back in the cupboard. Before he closes the door, I see that the cupboard is filled with photo frames. I see her face peeking out of another frame. 'Right, well, I'll take the hint and leave you boys alone then,' he says, instead of his normal jokey-type response. He leaves the room.

I look over to Dexter, and he's finally torn his eyes away from his laptop screen. He's looking at the door his dad walked out of with a scowl on his face.

'Do you guys have the thing of not putting up dead people's photos too then?' I ask, realising there are no photos of his mum around the house any more, even though there were loads when she was alive. 'I thought it was only Bengalis.'

'No, that's just Dad,' Dexter says, still staring at the door. 'He thinks that if he hides her photos in the cupboards, gives away all her stuff, removes every trace of her, then it'll be like she never existed.' He does a little scoff laugh, trying to shrug it off.

It's even more awkward now. I notice how he's completely changed. He's still looking at the door, but his hands are fists at his sides, and there's this expression on his face that I haven't seen before. Part angry, part . . . I want to say sad but I don't get why he'd be sad. He makes so many jokes about his dead mum, how could this have thrown him?

'I'm surprised you haven't added this to your material,' I say, spotting the charger on top of the cabinet next to me. 'Something about her being stuffed in that cupboard like a coffin.' I walk back over to the sofa with the charger, hand it to him.

He looks at me with the same scowl he had on for his dad, and it makes my heart jump. Is he mad at me? I guess it's OK for him to joke about his dead mum, but it's probably not right for me to do it, is it?

'Sorry,' I say, running a hand through my hair and tugging as I sit back down. 'That was a bad joke. I should have –'

'No, no, it's fine,' he says. The usual lightness not quite back into his voice. 'It's just . . . it's complicated.'

He doesn't continue. I know I should push him. I should ask him about it. It's what a good friend would do. It's what I should do. But . . . we don't talk about the deep stuff, me and Dexter.

Seeing his mum in that photo has reminded me of something though, and I can't help but blurt it out.

'Remember that time when she got super into trying to make dumplings? And she made like a dozen different kinds and made us be her taste testers? We sat in your dining room at that table for hours, watching her cook them, begging to help roll the dough out, but she wanted to do every single stage herself because she was following a recipe.'

'Oh my God,' Dexter laughs. 'I totally forgot about that. She was always trying to do new things in the kitchen. Before dumplings it was filled cupcakes.'

'I mean, I would have *gladly* been a taste tester for those,' I laugh.

'Man, I miss her,' he says quietly.

Oh God. I should console him, right? When Mariyam's sad, I give her a hug, but that's . . . that's not us. Dexter would probably think I was a freak if I tried to hug him. It's just such a weird situation. I've not seen him like this before. Sure, he was sad when his mum died, but he never really showed it. I never saw him cry, he never wanted to talk about it, instead just made bad jokes. Maybe that's the way forward, to distract him with jokes.

'I just wish –' he starts.

'And then we tried to learn how to use chopsticks, remember?' I say, accidentally cutting him off. 'Shit, sorry,' I say, 'You go,'

But before he can finish what he was going to say, he's interrupted by the sound of my phone ringing. I pull it out and see it's Ma.

'I'm just gonna . . .' I say, gesturing to the door. There's no way I can take a call from Ma in front of Dexter, no way I can speak Bengali in front of him. I leave the living room, stand in the hallway and answer the call, already worrying that there's something wrong. An accident, a fire, a death.

'Hello?'

'Ibrahim, where are you?' Ma asks, even though she knows where I am.

'What's happened? Is something wrong?'

'Come home now,' she says calmly. 'I need to go to Radiya's house. Your baba is still at work. Mariyam will be alone. Come watch her.'

'I'll be there in five minutes,' I tell her. There's no point trying to argue, trying to get some more time with Dexter, more time out of the house, more time being a normal teenager. Those things don't exist within our family.

I say a hasty goodbye to Dexter.

15

I wouldn't usually choose the living room to sit and work on my comedy stuff, but Ma's still at Auntie Radiya's, Baba's not back from work and Hamza texted to say he's going out with his friends after his football match, so I'm still babysitting, and I have no other choice but to be here while Mariyam is glued to the TV. I know I shouldn't let her just sit in front of it (usually when it's just me and her, I try and get to her to actually *do* things rather than be attached to a screen), but I'm really freaking out about the next stage of the competition. I try to be like Dexter, to just go with the flow and not stress about things until they're actually happening, but that's not how my brain works. There's no way I'll be able to stop obsessing about this until I have a plan, until I know how I'm going to go about it.

Dexter suggested watching some comedy shows that have a similar set-up, to get an idea of how they go. I've been watching clips of *Whose Line Is it Anyway?*, taking notes on what works, what doesn't go down so well.

'Bhaiyya!' Mariyam shouts, right in my ear that doesn't have an earbud in.

I turn to find she's sitting next to me on the sofa, whereas she was lying on the floor just a second ago. She's right up in my face.

'What?!' I ask angrily. 'Why are you shouting in my ear?'

'You weren't listening to me. I said I'm hungry!'

'Ma'll be back soon,' I tell her. 'She'll make dinner.' I turn back to my laptop, rewinding ten seconds to see what I missed.

'Can I get a snack?' Mariyam asks, making me rewind once again.

'Yeah, fine, whatever,' I say, trying not to shout at her.

She finally goes off and I put the volume louder on my laptop. I push the earbud further into my ear and press play. The host takes a slip of paper out of a hat and reads out a scenario. It takes the contestants like a second to get into it, to dive right in. No stumbling, no umms, no aahs. Just straight into comedy gold. How the hell do they do that?

There's a crash from the kitchen – the sound of a plastic biscuit jar falling to the ground. I roll my eyes and feel the anger rising up inside me.

'You better be cleaning that up!' I shout at Mariyam.

I think she says something back; I'm not paying enough attention. I know I should go and check on her, but the audience has just burst into laughter, and the host is laughing so hard he's flopped over the desk. I need to know what made them react like that. I need to do things that make people react like that. It's the only way I'll be able to get into the top three of the competition, to have a chance of winning a mentorship with an actual real-life comedian.

The front door opens as I'm rewinding the clip. I look up

and Baba walks in, phone in hand. I look back down to my screen, trying for the third time to watch this scene.

'Ibrahim, read this text,' he says in Bengali, right beside me now. Seriously, what's with my family and the lack of personal space?

'I'll look at it later,' I say, adjusting my earbud, trying to give him the hint. 'I'm busy.'

'You're not busy, you're just watching videos,' he says.

I turn to him then and realise that he's looking at my screen, seeing what I'm watching. I shut the laptop lid. 'It's nothing,' I say quickly. 'Just some research for school.'

Baba doesn't say anything, but he's still looking at my laptop.

Anxiety spikes in my chest. He can't have seen enough to know what it was, right? It's not like he'd ever think I was into something like comedy. In his eyes, people like us don't go into the world of entertainment. We become lawyers, accountants, doctors, or work in an Indian restaurant, like he does. I push my glasses up my nose and run my hand through my hair, tugging at it a bit.

'Just look,' he says, thrusting his phone at me.

I sigh and take it. I don't know why he bothers having a phone if he can't use it properly.

'It's from Royal Mail,' Baba says, looking over my shoulder. I feel his breath on my skin and recoil.

'There's a package for you,' I say, skimming the text and quickly handing it back to him so he'll move away. 'You just need to confirm your details.'

'Oh!' he says suddenly. 'Maybe it's those slippers I ordered for your ma.'

'That'll be it,' I say, desperate to get back to my research.

Baba takes out his wallet and starts tapping away on his phone as he walks into the kitchen.

I grab my laptop and headphones and go up to my room. Baba's here to look after Mariyam now, and I need to get into shape for the next round of the competition. I have some serious work to do.

16

Ma's made chicken biryani for dinner, which I would usually love, but I'm in a bad mood. I barely got to watch any of the clips I had wanted to before Baba called me down to fix the TV after he accidentally put Spanish subtitles on. And to make things worse, Mariyam is being a right little brat today.

'You're a big girl now,' I tell her. 'You should be feeding yourself.' I grumpily hold out a spoonful of food to her.

She scrunches up her face, crosses her arms and refuses to open her mouth.

'Oh God, c'mon, Mariyam, please. Your food's getting cold. *My* food is getting cold.'

'I don't want it!' she protests.

I look over to Ma, hoping she'll jump in and take over, as she normally does when Mariyam is being this fussy, but she's just looking down at her mobile. Honestly, what is it with my parents and their phones today?

'Did you pay my mobile bill?' Ma asks Baba.

He looks up from his plate. 'It goes out automatically every month, right, Ibrahim?'

I suck in a breath and nod my head. This type of thing gets

97

to me when I'm already stressed. All I can think about is how no one else I know has to deal with this. No one else's parents ask them to read texts for them, ask them simple things like how their bills work. Everyone else's parents seem to be able to adult with ease. And then to have my own crap on top of that, upcoming GCSEs, the stress of the competition, and now possibly a mental illness too?

I know, in the scheme of things, it's not a huge deal. I mean, my parents manage to get by, day to day. The house hasn't been repossessed or anything – yet. And I know I'm being harsh on them. I need to take into account the circumstances – how they came to a completely new country and had to learn everything themselves. And also that they're just doing things the way they were brought up, how things are in our culture. But . . . at times it gets to me a lot. It makes me feel all stressed and angry, and I can sense the bad feelings already rolling around inside of me.

'Are you sure?' Ma asks. 'I've been trying to call Radiya all day and it's not working.'

'How do I check, Ibrahim?' Baba asks. He can see I'm still trying to get this spoon of food into Mariyam's mouth, he can see Hamza sitting right next to him, but still he won't ask him. It always lands on me.

'Just check your bank app,' I tell Baba, finally managing to slip the food into Mariyam's mouth as she's distracted by the conversation. 'It will show you all the recent transactions. You can see if the money's been taken.'

'What app?' Baba asks, getting out his phone. He stares at it, confused, as he flicks through the screens.

'Ugh, give it here, I'll do it.' I say, taking the phone out of his hand.

I open Baba's banking app, put in the passcode he chose but probably doesn't even remember. And . . . no, wait. This can't be right. There were thousands in this account when I checked the other day.

'There's no money in the account,' I say, looking up at him.

'What?' he exclaims, looking up from his plate. 'You must be looking at *your* account.'

'No, Baba,' I say, not having the energy to ask why my account would be on his phone. 'Definitely on your account.' I flick to the recent transactions page. Maybe all the bills went out at the same time, or maybe his wages haven't come in yet. There must be a reason, right? Crap – is it something I did? Did I accidentally click a button or something? I'm the only one who uses his online banking app, so it must be me, right?

I scan the list of recent transactions desperately until my eyes fall on the one at the top. Over seven thousand pounds transferred to an account just today.

'It says you sent all your money to someone today,' I tell Baba. I can feel my heart pounding in my chest, the blood rushing to my head, making me feel a bit dizzy.

'What?! No! I haven't sent anyone anything,' Baba says. He gets up and comes over, looking at the screen over my shoulder, as if I might be making this all up. I close the app and open it up again, just in case it's a glitch or something. But no, once again, right at the top is that huge transaction, shouting out to me like a siren. The balance above reads zero. Panic courses through my body.

'Well, it definitely shows here that you transferred all this money to someone. Did you enter your account details anywhere? Have you used your card today? Though I don't think you can spend that much on your card alone.'

'The only thing I've done today was pay for that parcel from Royal Mail,' he says. 'Remember, I showed you it earlier? They said they'll deliver it next week. But that was only a few pounds. Not thousands.'

Shit.

No way, no way, no way.

I quickly go into his texts, looking at the one at the top. It does indeed say it's from Royal Mail, but there's no space between the words like there should be, and it's all in lower case. The message itself does seem legit. The words are spelled right and make sense. But then I look at the link. That is definitely *not* a legit link to the Royal Mail website. I click on it anyway, because at this point what worse could happen, and the website is just so poorly designed. The Royal Mail logo is blurry as fuck, and everything looks out of kilter and . . . wrong.

'Oh my God,' I say. 'How did you not realise this was fake?!'

'I showed you, and you said it was fine!' Baba says. 'You told me to go ahead and put my details in.'

He's right. I did. This is all my fault. I was being selfish, trying to prepare for something I wanted to do, something only for me. All I had to do was spare a minute of my time to read this properly. I would have seen right away that the link wasn't real, if I was paying attention. I would have prevented us losing all this money.

The panic is rising inside me now. The weird, horrible feeling in my chest starts up. The constricting, the tightening, the feeling that any second now I'm about to crumble completely.

'Ibrahim, you have to call the bank!' Baba says, desperately. 'Call them now. They can stop it, right? Get the money back?'

'I . . . I don't know,' I say through shaky breaths. 'You . . . You put your details in yourself. I don't know if they'll give you it back if it was . . . technically your fault . . .'

'But it wasn't his fault!' Ma pipes up. 'The people tricked him. Just call the bank and explain it.'

'Call them,' Baba repeats. 'Call them now!' There's so much panic in his voice that it cuts at my brain. I've never seen him in such a state, this panicked. He's so worried, so scared he's lost all of our savings. And it's all my fault.

The panic attack is here now, I can feel my breaths coming out in shaky shudders, can feel my heart about to give up. I'm going to collapse. Right here, right now. In front of everyone. But Baba is relying on me to fix this. I need to fix this. This is my fault. I need to put it right.

I force myself to take some deep breaths, even though I probably look like a total idiot. But that doesn't matter right now. I need to fix this. That's the most important thing.

I get up off my chair, my jelly legs nearly letting me flop to the ground in the process. But I need some distance from my family at least. I go to the corner of the room, my shaky fingers googling the number for the bank's customer services.

No such thing as distance though, as Baba follows right behind me, crowding my space, making me feel even more trapped, more desperate for release, for this panic attack to be over already.

Breathe, Ibrahim, breathe. You can do this. Focus on finding this number. Focus your eyes. Focus your damn eyes! I can't let my weakness get in the way of putting it right. I try and force the feelings away, try and force my body to be normal, or at least seem normal from the outside.

Baba doesn't say anything about my breathing, or shaking, even though I'm pretty sure it's obvious. So maybe I'm pulling it off. Or maybe he just doesn't care.

Being on hold isn't helping things at all. Every thirty seconds or so, the cheesy music clicks as if someone is picking up the call, which makes my heart rate spike even more, causing the panic attack to worsen, before the music starts playing again.

When someone *does* finally pick up, I'm already sweating through my T-shirt.

'H-hello?' I say in a shaky breath when the phone clicks for real this time.

'Good evening, this is Lesley speaking, how can I help?'

She sounds fed up.

'Hello?' she says again, impatiently.

I force myself to sound normal, to regulate my breaths and not let on what a stupid pathetic mess I am.

'Yes, sorry, hello,' I say quickly.

'Tell her the Royal Mail are stealing our money,' Baba tries to whisper in my ear. I shrug him off, and turn away to face into the corner of the room, hoping he'll take the hint.

'How can I help?' the woman asks again.

I explain the situation to her, telling her about the dodgy-looking link, and how Baba believed it was real and put his details in.

'Are you the account holder?' she asks.

'No, I'm speaking on behalf of my father. Do you need him to confirm it's OK for you to talk to me?' I know how it goes, know the procedures, the right things to say. Usually the people on the other end are understanding of the situation and just need Baba to confirm his details, and that he's happy for them to talk to me.

But not Lesley.

'I'm sorry, I can only discuss these details with the account holder himself. May I speak to Mr Abdul Malik, please?'

'Yeah, sure,' I say, grateful for a break to try to stop my heart racing so much, but also sure that putting Baba on won't help the situation. My anxiety is through the roof.

As expected, the conversation between Baba and Lesley does not go smoothly. He confirms his personal and account details, then recounts his version of what happened in broken English. I can hear Lesley's asking questions, but I can't make out the words. Baba's answers consist of 'Huh?' And 'What?' And 'I don't understand'.

'Talk to my son,' he says. He thrusts the phone back towards me, even though Lesley is clearly still talking.

I shouldn't have to be in this position! I mean, I'm sixteen, for fuck's sake. What other sixteen-year-olds have to talk to the bank on behalf of their father? These kinds of situations make me wonder how my parents would ever cope without me here.

Well, I guess if I weren't here, they wouldn't be in this mess in the first place.

'I'm sorry, but I can only discuss this with the account holder,' Lesley says again. Her voice is dripping with impatience now.

'He's just said it's OK for you to talk to me about it,' I explain, trying not to sound just as impatient. 'His English isn't great. It would just be easier for you to deal with me. I can relay all the information back to him. He's still in the room.'

'I'm sorry, without a letter of authority on the file this goes against our company policy.'

There's a stabbing pain in my chest, as if my heart is now suddenly completely blocked, entirely stopped.

'B-but . . .' I manage to splutter, 'we've . . . we've done this before.'

'I've frozen the account for the time being,' Lesley says, ignoring me completely. 'I'll pass your father's information on to the fraud team, but unfortunately this is something he is going to have to deal with himself.'

'So, wait,' I say, barely managing to get the words out. 'What . . . what do we do now?'

She takes a deep angry breath through her nose. 'As I said, I will be passing this issue on to the fraud team, and they'll be in touch. In the meantime, the account will be frozen so no more money can come in or go out. I have to leave it up to the fraud team, as it's their area. That's all I can do for you today.'

There's a sense of finality in her voice. No sympathy or empathy at all. I've annoyed her too.

This is all my fault.

'What are we going to do?' Ma whispers when the call ends. 'If they can't get it back,' she adds, 'what are we going to do? How are we going to pay the bills?'

Baba doesn't answer. He can't even meet her eye. Their faces . . . both of them . . . they're . . . devastated.

And it's all because of me. If we don't get this money back, we'll be . . . we'll be screwed. I look from Baba to Ma, their faces filled with worry, and feel my chest tighten.

I'm about to collapse.

This panic attack is about to reach its peak.

They can't see me like this. They'll worry. As if they don't have enough to worry about already. And all because of me. I always make them worry. I always make things worse for them. I bet they wish I'd never been born.

Everything is my fault.

I need to get out of here.

I get up off my chair, trying to act as normal as possible.

I sneak out of the dining room, willing my body not to collapse just yet.

I open the front door.

I need to get away from this.

They're better with me as far away as possible.

I close the door quietly behind me and then I run.

17

Sura. I need Sura.

She'll know how to stop this. The only thing I know that for sure makes it stop is Sura. Every time I've gone to her when I'm feeling like this, she's made it better.

I try . . . I really do try to use her technique of rational thinking. But there's no room in my brain to form those thoughts. My mind is just filled with an angry buzzing of self-loathing and hatred, and guilt. So much guilt.

The one thought looping around my head is that my family's lost everything and it's all my fault.

I blindly stumble my way to the community centre. I don't remember the journey at all. One of the perks of it being so close, I guess, I can get there without even trying, without paying attention, without being able to see straight or hear clearly.

I stumble up the path to the door, knowing that if anyone saw me they'd probably call the police because I'm being such a weirdo, but also not caring because I just need this to be over. I need Sura to make this stop. She's the only one who can help me.

I pull on the door with the tiny bit of strength I have in me. But it doesn't budge.

Of course. It's locked.

Fuck.

What the hell do I do now? How else can I get to Sura? I know she's, like, magic of some sort, so can I just summon her? Do a little dance, click my heels together and sing her name?

Gah! I need to get inside.

I pull on the door harder, as hard as I can, but it doesn't even rattle. It's not the kind of lock I can break with a kick, like they do in all the films, not that I'd be able to with how weak my body is right now. I look around, hoping a window has been left open, but nothing. I know there's a back entrance, so I go around the building to the door by the car park. It's darker here. And much dirtier. The door looks flimsier. But it's also locked. Fuck fuck fuck.

Wait. No. I think this is one of those doors that locks when you close it, but can be opened from the inside. If I could just get to the handle on the inside . . .

There's no other way . . .

I'm desperate, and the only thing standing between me now and me not dying is this door with a glass window pane. I frantically look around for something to break the glass with. A part of me knows how wrong this is, but that goes out of the window (no pun intended) when I'm feeling this absolutely desperate.

Ah! A rock. Thank fuck.

I pick it up and smash it against the window with all the strength I can muster.

The noise isn't as loud as I thought it would be, but then again, my ears feel blocked, the way they always do when I'm panicking. I carefully reach in, over the spikes of glass, to the side I know the handle is at. I reach around for the handle for a few seconds, getting more and more desperate when I can't find it. If I can't get in . . . if I can't find Sura . . . I don't know what will happen to me. Whether this panic attack will ever end. At least not without ending me too.

Thankfully, I find the handle and . . . yes! The door opens. I pull my hand back out, carefully avoiding the sharp glass. As soon as the door's open, I'm in and running. Running to the back room. The panic is getting worse and worse every step and I'm genuinely terrified I might not make it. That I might just collapse and die right here in the grotty community-centre corridor. What a way to go.

I want to scream out for her. For her to come find me and work her magic, but there's barely enough air inside me to breathe, let alone scream. As I burst through the door to the back room, there are black spots in my vision.

I can't stand this. I can't I can't I can't.

It needs to stop. Even if it means . . .

'Hey, Ibrahim. Deep breaths.' I hear faintly, through the incessant buzzing in my head.

I open my eyes and I'm on the ground, curled up on the carpet, and looking up at her.

She's blurry, but she's here.

Sura's here.

It's going to be OK.

She'll make it OK.

18

Sura kneels on the floor in front of me, doing her deep-breathing thing. I just sit there, back against the wall, knees up with arms around them, and breathe in time with her, though my breaths are way more shaky than hers. My entire body is trembling, and the air rattles in and out of my lungs. But my vision is clearer. I can see her properly. The electric-blue scarf and polka-dot dress that she always wears. The kindness in her eyes is there too, but today there also seems to be a hint of pity, and this infuriates me.

As soon as my breathing is almost completely back to normal, I unclench my body and sit cross-legged in front of her. She smiles at me, as if this is a sign that I'm back to normal, but I scowl at her. This makes her smile drop a little. Good.

'Why is this happening?' I shout at her. 'You told me the panic attacks would stop. You *promised* they would stop, and yet here we are. That was the worst one yet.'

Part of me wants my words to hurt her, for her to feel something of what I am going through right now, but my anger doesn't seem to register in her expression. She looks just as calm and kind as ever.

'I gave you a few techniques to *help*,' she says softly. 'I never said they would stop the panic attacks completely. It's not a magical cure. The only thing that can stop them completely is to deal with the issues causing them in the first place.'

'I told you I'm not going to go to a fucking therapist! Talking about this isn't going to help – otherwise they'd have stopped after I talked about them to you.'

'I'm not a trained professional, Ibrahim. You came here today because you wanted me to help you. I mean, *you* broke a window. That's how much you wanted to get help. Why is it OK to accept help from *me* but not from a therapist, someone whose job it literally is to help you? Someone who would be able to help you manage your feelings. I can't promise they'll make the panic attacks go away completely, but –'

'No!' I cut her preaching off. 'I'm not going to a fucking therapist. I don't need one. I don't need anyone's help. I'm *beyond* help. I'm the thing that shouldn't be here. I can't be fixed.' Somehow I've started crying, and can feel my heart hurting from my words. The truth that's coming out of me.

'Everyone would be better off without me,' I say, a bit quieter. 'They'd be so much better off if I had never been born.'

'Do you really believe that?'

'Of course,' I reply quickly. 'Just think about how much better off my family would be if I wasn't there to screw things up. If I wasn't there to tell Baba to fall for scams that steal all our money. I make everything worse, Sura. Everyone I meet . . . I ruin things. I'm the problem. I can't do anything right. I can't . . . They'd all be better off without me.'

'Well, I think you're wrong,' she says, strong, determined.

110

I look up at her, wipe my nose with the back of my hand. 'You don't know . . .' I whisper.

'Oh, but I do,' she says. 'And I can prove it.'

'What do you mean?' I ask, lifting my glasses up to wipe my eyes.

'Magic, remember?' she says. 'I can show you the truth.'

'What truth?' I scoff, putting my glasses back. 'The truth has been in front of me all along. I saw the look on Ma's face earlier, worrying about how they're going to pay the mortgage, pay the bills. If we lose the house, it's going to be my fault. That's the truth. You can't deny that.'

'Well, actually, I can,' she says, rearranging herself so she's sitting cross-legged too now. 'Rational thinking, remember? This wasn't your fault. You didn't *make* your father enter his card details into that website. You didn't create the scam that stole from him. It wasn't your doing, but I know you're not in a place to believe that right now. So let's try something else.'

'What else?' I ask. I shouldn't let her get to me, I know. But last time . . . her words really helped last time. And I'm desperate right now.

'You believe so strongly that you haven't had a positive impact on anyone's life. But I can show you for a fact that's not true. I can show you something good that's happening literally right this minute all because of you.'

Well, that's piqued my curiosity. 'So where are we going?' I ask, putting my palms down on the carpet to get up.

She reaches over and pushes me back down by the shoulder. 'No need to get up. Magic, remember?' She's smirking now, and I can't help but roll my eyes. 'I can show you from right here.'

I'm intrigued, but also worried it won't work. What if I've gotten to the stage where I can't be helped any more?

'And what exactly are you going to show me?' I ask.

She grins at me. 'Just close your eyes and let me take you to a scene that's happening right now. Like, literally this second. A scene that will prove you've had a good impact.'

I take a deep breath, preparing myself. I close my eyes.

19

We're in Dexter's living room. The TV's on and Mr Murgen is sitting on the sofa.

OK, I was definitely not expecting this.

'Why are we in Dexter's house?' I ask, confused. I feel the need to whisper, as if Mr Murgen might hear us. I was expecting Sura to take me home, for her to show me my family worried sick about where I've run off to, to see them rejoicing about the fact the money has just suddenly appeared back in Baba's account. But instead I'm standing against the wall, watching Dexter's dad flicking through a news website on his phone.

'You were here earlier, right?' Sura asks.

'Yeah,' I reply. 'I was hanging with Dexter.'

'Do you remember what you talked about?'

I make a face at her. 'We were . . . I dunno. We talk about a lot of stuff. I don't remember. Why are you asking these weird questions? Just tell me what your point is.'

She sighs dramatically. 'I can't do *everything* for you, Ibrahim. Maybe just watch and see if you can figure it out.' She gestures to the door with her chin. A second later, it opens, and Dexter walks in. He looks in our direction and panic jolts in my chest.

'Can he see us?' I whisper to Sura, shuffling on the spot, trying to hide behind her.

'Yeah, he can,' she replies. She waves to him.

Shit. Fuck. What the hell? How am I meant to explain any of this to him?

'Oh God, um . . . Dexter, it's not . . .'

Sura doesn't even last three seconds before she's full-on cackling. Dexter's not looking our way any more. He's looking at his dad on the sofa.

'Oh my God, you're evil,' I say, pressing a hand to my chest, where I can feel my heart pounding.

'Sorry,' she splutters. 'I couldn't help it.'

I shake my head, but I'm smiling too.

Mr Murgen looks up and spots Dexter. 'Oh, didn't hear you come in,' he says. 'Did you want to watch something?' He offers Dexter the remote.

Dexter doesn't take it. There's a look on his face that I've not seen before. He's normally in such good spirits, always a smile on his face, but now he just looks . . . I don't want to say sad, though there is a bit of that in his expression. He just seems . . . different. Serious.

'No,' he replies. His voice is quieter than usual, but it's determined. His posture is determined too. He looks back over in our direction, and my heart lurches again, but then I see he's actually looking at the cupboard next to us. He walks over to it and opens the same door that I opened earlier. This time, nothing falls out. Instead, Dexter reaches in and pulls out the photo frame, the one with the picture of his mother that I broke earlier. Dexter stands looking at the photo for a few seconds. A small smile appears on his face as he runs this thumb over the glass, avoiding the big crack in the middle.

'Everything OK, son?' Mr Murgen asks slowly, carefully. He's probably as weirded out as I am by Dexter's behaviour. Or maybe this is what he's like at home. Maybe, like me, he puts on a face at school and around other people. But what would be the need? His dad is normal. His house is normal. He's got no reason to pretend. And yet . . . I've known him for years and never seen him as serious as this.

'No,' Dexter replies. 'Everything *isn't* OK.' He turns to face his dad, and there's . . . tears in his eyes. Dexter's crying? What's happened? It can't have been from just looking at his mother's photo, could it? He makes so many jokes about her, I thought he was . . . I thought he'd gotten over her death. I just assumed everything was OK.

'What . . . are you doing with that?' Mr Murgen asks, looking at the frame in Dexter's hand. His voice is quieter now too. As if he's scared of what Dexter's answer might be.

'Ibrahim made a comment earlier,' Dexter says, striking fear into my heart. Fuck! That's why he's crying – because of me. *This* is what Sura thought would help?!

'About how we keep Mum locked up in the cupboards like a coffin. And he's right, y'know. Why . . . why *do* we hide all her photos?' He turns to his father, who seems lost for words.

Mr Murgen stands up. He walks over to Dexter, and I think he might hug him, but instead he takes the frame out of his hands softly. He doesn't even look at the photo before opening the cabinet and stuffing it back in there. He shuts the door a bit too hard and the noise echoes around the room.

115

'Your mother's gone,' he says stiffly. 'There's no point us dwelling on it. Now, come on, shall we order –'

'No point *dwelling on it*?' Dexter half screams. 'She . . . she *died*, Dad. My mother died. And you're . . . you're just shoving her in a cupboard like she never even mattered in the first place. Like she never even *existed*.' He yanks open the cupboard and pulls out the same photo frame again. He slams it on display on top of the cabinet so hard I think the frame cracks a bit more. Then he pulls out another frame. Another photo of his mother, this one holding a tiny baby Dexter. He puts this one on display too, and goes to reach in for another one, but Mr Murgen grabs his hand.

'Dexter, what are you doing?!'

'I'm remembering Mum!' Dexter screams. Full-on screams now. 'I know you've gotten over her, or whatever. But I haven't, OK? I miss her. Every fucking day I miss her. And I want to see her. I want to remember what she looked like. I want there to be photos of her around the house like there were when she was alive. Surely it's *more* important to have them up now that she's gone? I don't get it, Dad. Why are you just hiding her away, giving away her things or putting them in the loft? Why are you trying to erase her from our lives? Today, when Ibrahim brought her up, it was the first time I've spoken to someone about her in . . . in a *long* time. And that was from my friend, not you. My *friend* talks about her more than you do. What does that say, Dad?'

Dexter runs out of steam, stands there breathing hard, looking at his dad, waiting. Mr Murgen is just standing there too, but his head is down slightly. He can't meet Dexter's gaze.

'Well?' Dexter prompts after a few seconds of silence. 'Are you going to say something? Or are you just going to keep brushing things under the carpet? Pretending my feelings don't exist? Pretending *she* never existed?'

He's got tears streaming down his face now. Snot too. I've never seen him this upset, this emotional. It's breaking my heart a little bit to know he's had these horrible feelings bottled up inside him. I guess I relate a little. It's weird seeing him like this, because it's so unlike him. Or the version of him I know, anyway. But it makes me feel a bit guilty too, because . . . I've been here. All this time. I was there when his mum died. I was at his house every week after that. I should have seen how much he was hurting. Best friends should notice these things.

I run a hand through my hair, tug on it. I think Sura notices, because she glances at me. She opens her mouth to say something, and I'm scared she's going to say the same thing that's running through my head. That I should have helped Dexter through this. But before she can say anything, Mr Murgen pipes up.

'I just . . . thought it would be better . . .' he says quietly. 'Less painful.'

He and Dexter finally lock eyes. Sadness fills their gaze.

'For you, maybe,' Dexter bites. 'But not . . . not for me.'

Silence again. I feel like I'm intruding on a super-private family moment, but I'm also desperate to see what happens next.

'Do you even miss her?' Dexter asks, spite lacing his tone. 'Or were you glad when she died?'

'Of course I miss her!' Mr Murgen booms back. The intensity

of his words makes Dexter's eyes widen, and I jump a little, shocked. 'How can you even ask that?' Mr Murgen's crying too now. 'Your mum . . . she was the love of my life, Dexter. I was *devastated* when she died. I still am. Of course I am. She was an amazing woman. And it just . . . it hurts so much. I miss her so much. So, yes, OK, maybe part of me thought that if I put away all of the photos, donated the apron she wore every Sunday to make pancakes, got rid of even the smell of her perfume around the house, that maybe . . . just maybe, it would be easier to cope with it all.'

'You seem to have been coping just fine,' Dexter spits. But he's quieter now, as if the fight is running out of him. 'Every time I see you you're just . . . smiling . . . laughing . . .'

'And you're not?' Mr Murgen asks. He pierces Dexter with his glare. 'I had no idea you felt like this, son,' he says, his posture sagging a little. 'You always just seemed so . . . OK. I thought . . . I thought you were coping. If I'd known . . .' They both look at each other, both with tears streaming down their faces. And then Mr Murgen steps towards Dexter and wraps him into a tight hug. I see surprise bloom on Dexter's face, and he takes a second, but he wraps his arms around his dad too.

'How about we both agree to talk about things more?' Mr Murgen suggests.

'Sure thing, Dad,' Dexter says. 'As long as you don't talk to me about boring things, like . . . your life or hobbies or whatever.'

Mr Murgen lets out a throaty laugh, and clutches Dexter tighter. 'Why don't we go up to the loft and see what stuff of your mother's you'd like to keep?'

'Sounds good.'

118

'You know I love you, right, Dexter?' Mr Murgen says, pulling out of the hug, but holding Dexter by his shoulders, smiling down at him.

I wait to see what joke Dexter comes out with, but surprisingly, all he does is smile and say, 'I love you too.'

I lift my glasses up and rub the tears out of my eyes. When my vision returns back to normal, I see I'm back in the community centre, with Sura sitting in front of me, a wide grin on her face.

20

'Well?' Sura asks.

'Well, what?' I ask, still trying to get used to the whole teleporting business. 'You said you were going to show me proof that . . . that I don't ruin people's lives, and instead, you showed me . . . Dexter and his dad?'

'I told you I was going to show you something happening right now that was a result of your positive influence.'

I cock an eyebrow at her. 'That wasn't me. That was all Dexter and his dad. I had . . . nothing to do with that.'

'Now that's where you're wrong,' she says chirpily. She crosses her legs and scooches closer to me. 'That whole scene, that conversation, happened because of something *you* started. Dexter said himself that you talking about his mother sparked his decision to speak to his dad about it. You saw, right? How hard that was for him. You could tell how much it was eating at him.'

The image of Dexter's distraught face comes into my mind.

'A small thing,' Sura continues. 'That's all it takes, Ibrahim. To make a big difference. To have a positive impact. The things we do . . . they don't have to be huge to have a life-changing effect. You were there for Dexter. You let him talk about his mother. You remembered her, mentioned her. To you it might seem like nothing. You didn't know it would mean so much to him, sure. But it did. It made a difference, Ibrahim. It made *such* a difference.'

I try and take in what she's saying. Try to really listen to her words. She's speaking without the usual pep in her voice, so I know she's being serious, that this is something she really wants me to take in.

'Ibrahim, you do so many things. So many positive things. You're a good person, so it comes to you naturally and you don't even realise. The way you make your family laugh when they need a light moment, the way you make sure Mariyam speaks Bengali at home so that she doesn't forget it like some of your younger cousins, the way you sometimes practise shootouts with Hamza in the garden so he feels confident before his matches. These things . . . Ibrahim, they might seem like nothing to you, but they matter. They have an impact on other people. In *such* a good way. You matter, Ibrahim. Your family, your friends, the world is better with you in it, I promise. You've impacted people in ways you will . . . never know. You've made such a difference. You've made so many people's lives better. Even if it's in ways you can't see. But that doesn't make it any less true. Or any less meaningful. You make things better, Ibrahim. I promise.'

I'm weeping now. My heart's skipping, but in a good way. I'm so full of emotion. Listening to her words. Feeling the force of what she's saying. Because, yes, she's right. It's not only big things that make a difference. I've encountered that in my own life. How one small thing can make a huge change. Like Sura

121

coming into my life. Like Baba's text leading to the loss of all his savings. If that can lead to such a huge mess, surely the opposite can be true. Small good things can have a big impact too.

'It's just . . . so hard,' I tell her. 'It's like . . . like I have to be a parent to my parents. And I'm just . . . I'm not equipped for that. I never know whether I'm doing the right thing, or whether what I do is going to have a huge impact in a bad way, like with the scam text today. It's just . . . so much pressure, y'know? I'm always terrified of doing something irreversibly wrong, something that will ruin my whole family. My parents, they . . . they put so much faith in me. I guess they have no other choice, since I'm the oldest, but they just . . . don't understand how much pressure it puts on me. And no, before you ask, I can't talk to them about it. How even would I? We're not . . . we're not like Dexter and his dad. We're not like white families. We don't . . . we don't show our emotions, we don't talk about our feelings. And sure, maybe that's wrong, or whatever. But it's . . . it's the way our culture is. And there's no way to change that. No way could I just go up to my parents and blurt it out like I'm blurting it out to you. It's not . . . it's just not how things work. Your family must be the same?'

She averts her gaze as I ask this, and I see a sad look flit across her face before she plasters a smile back on, but it looks forced.

'I know our culture isn't great at this sort of thing,' she says, ignoring my question. 'But you shouldn't have to bear all this weight on your shoulders, Ibrahim. I know there seems like no way around it, but you can get help.'

I open my mouth to protest, but she chimes in, 'Not from a therapist!' She laughs a little. 'I meant, like, with the admin side of things. Help with finances. You could enrol your parents in an English class. There are courses available to help immigrants acclimate to life in the UK. There's so many options. They can't always rely on you to do everything. They need to learn to be independent.'

'It's not their fault,' I say quickly, pushing my glasses up my nose. 'It can't be easy . . . starting a new life in a new country, trying to assimilate. A new language, new rules. The fact they managed it at all is amazing. Like, they've done all the hard stuff, really. Getting us set up. And now, if I can help out in small ways, then surely it's my duty to. I mean, not like just out of obligation. But it's . . . like, they've done so much for me, I feel like I should repay the favour.'

'It's not a *favour*, Ibrahim. They're your parents. It's their *job* to look after you. You don't owe them anything in return for that. You didn't ask to be born.'

'No, no, I don't mean like that,' I say defensively. I run a hand through my hair and tug at it. 'I just mean like . . . in the scheme of things, it's not that much, you know? What they ask me to do – it's no big deal.'

Sura snorts a little. 'No big deal?! Right. That's why you're having regular panic attacks.' She sighs a little, pierces me with her stare. Only now do I realise her eyes are watery too. 'Look, Ibrahim, things need to change. You know that. *I* know that. You can't keep on carrying this weight. The guilt, the pressure. It's going to consume you. It already is. I get that you want to help your parents, your family. And I do agree that our culture puts a lot of pressure on the eldest child, especially in your circumstances. But . . . you need to live for yourself, Ibrahim. You can't carry on doing everything for other people, putting everyone over yourself. I know it may seem selfish, but why is that a bad thing? Why is it a bad thing to put your needs, your *health*, above the happiness of others? You said earlier that your parents managed when they first came over, right? Before you were old enough to help. Well, surely that proves that they *are* capable of doing these things themselves. It seems like they've just come to rely on you because you offer, or because it's easier when you do it. But that doesn't mean *only* you can do it.'

She's right. I know she is. 'It makes sense,' I say, pushing my glasses up. 'But it's just . . . it's not easy.'

'Change never is.' She shrugs. 'It's uncomfortable too, and I think that's the big thing here. You and your family are so comfortable in the way things have become, you don't want to change, even though you know, deep down, that you *could*. And maybe this is the breaking point for you. Maybe this can be the moment you set the wheels in motion to change your family for the better. Change your life for the better. You can do it, Ibrahim. I know you can.'

I look down to the dirty green carpet, feeling a blush come through me at her words. I can't stand it when people say nice things about me, to me. Especially not when they're this deep.

'I think it might help you to try to do something just for yourself at least once a day. It doesn't have to be big, just something where you're prioritising yourself without feeling guilty about it. And, ooh! Have you tried meditation? That works wonders for me –'

'Pfft,' I say, rolling my eyes. 'All that sitting around, humming. How is that helpful?'

'That's not what meditation is!' Sura protests. 'It's more about –'

'Hard pass on meditation,' I say forcefully. There's no way I'm doing any of that crap. It's bad enough with the breathing techniques. If someone saw me doing the whole closed eyes, deep-thinking crap, they'd think I was a complete pussy. 'The thing you taught me the other day though, the evidence thing, that works well. I like that. I like how it can sort of quickly change the way I'm feeling, the way I'm thinking.'

'Good! I'm glad something's working for you. Another thing that can help is to just focus on the next step. You're one of those people who's always looking five steps ahead. Always catastrophising. It's what causes a lot of your anxiety. A way to combat that is to live in the moment. Try and focus on literally your next move. Saying it out loud can help too, when you're in the middle of a panic attack. Just like, "I am going to go into the kitchen", "I am going to get a glass of water", "I am going to tell Sura she's a genius."'

I roll my eyes, but a little laugh pops out too.

'Taking your brain away from the negativity and focusing it instead on just the present and what you're going to do right now is a good way of easing the panic.'

'Not sure about saying it out loud, or the you being a genius part,' I say. 'But the idea of being in the present sounds like it might work. I'll give it a whirl next time I need it.'

She grins. 'And come back to me whenever you need help,' she says. 'You know where I am. Find a way, like you did today. Maybe less vandalism next time. There's a spare key hidden in a fake black rock near the front door. Whenever you need me. I'm here for you.'

'Why?' I blurt, needing to know more about her, why she's here, if she's even real. 'Why do you even want to help me so much? Who am I to you?'

Her mask slips, and there's a flicker of panic in her eyes, as if I've almost stumbled on her secret.

My heart races, thinking she's about to tell me, about to reveal her truth, answer all the questions that have been tumbling about in my head since I first met her.

She plasters on a warm smile, and there's still a tiny hope in me that, considering I've bared my soul to her, that she will give me *something* in return.

'Someone helped me when I was in your position,' she says guardedly. 'I want to . . . I want to do the same.' She shrugs.

'Tell me about it?' I ask, hoping she'll indulge me, but knowing deep down she either likes or needs to have this mysterious air about her.

'You should get back to your family,' she says instead, ignoring me once again. 'They're starting to wonder where you went.'

Shit.

She's right. I look up at the clock on the wall. I don't know when I left, or how long it's been since I ran out. I don't even have my phone if they're trying to call. They must be worried sick. I left them at such a bad time.

But I needed to.

I needed this.

I needed Sura.

'One day you've got to tell me *something* about yourself,' I say.

'One day,' she says with a smile.

21

I expect Ma and Baba to be either out of their minds with worry, or not have realised I was missing at all. But the reality is somewhere in the middle. They're in the living room, but they're sitting down, instead of pacing about like they were when I left. They've got cups of tea in front of them, and they've actually drunk them, so they must be feeling a *bit* better. Like they say, a cup of tea can fix anything. (And people accuse my parents of not being 'British enough'.)

They both look up when I enter the room.

'Ibrahim, where did you go?' Ma asks. There's no panic in her voice. Still a tinge of stress, but not the overwhelming 'our life is about to end' state that she was in when I got off the phone with the bank earlier.

'Oh. I . . . I . . .' God, a whole five-minute walk back and I didn't think to even come up with a reasonable excuse for just legging it out of the door without a word. 'I just . . . needed to do something,' I say. 'Did the bank call back?' I ask, hoping to distract them both enough so I don't have to tell them how I just broke into the community centre to see a girl who may or may not be a figment of my imagination.

'The fraud team called,' Baba says, pressing a button on his phone so the screen illuminates. He looks down at it. 'They said it's a scam that's been going around. It wasn't really the Royal Mail, can you believe it? Who does that? Anyway, they said they can get the money back in the account in a few days. Can you check the app?'

He looks up at me from his seat on the sofa, and oh my God the relief that flows through me, seeing the lack of stress on his face! I almost fall over from it. I feel my legs actually going a bit weak, so I go and sit down next to Baba, taking the phone from him, because I know he means he wants me to check the app now, even though the money isn't due back for a few days.

'Maaaaaaaa!' Mariyam calls from upstairs.

'What?' she shouts back, not moving from her seat.

'Which way does the prayer mat go?'

'I showed you the other day!' Ma shouts, still unmoving. 'Diagonally towards the wardrobe.'

'I don't understand what you mean,' Mariyam calls back, unable to understand Ma's Bengali directions.

Ma mutters under her breath, 'So desperate to grow up, she only wants to pray on her own.' She gets up, grabs the empty cups and leaves the room.

The cold air of the door closing hits me, makes me shiver. It's part a normal reaction, and part just adrenaline, I guess, from knowing that everything is going to be OK. The money will be back in the account. We won't lose the house, or the car. We'll be OK. Just like Sura said.

'It's not back yet,' I tell Baba as the app finally loads. 'It still says the account is frozen too.'

128

'Hmm, OK, fine,' he says, deflated. 'At least no bills are going out in the next few days. There shouldn't be any problems inshallah.'

I'm shocked he knows when the bills go out. I didn't think he paid that much attention, considering he doesn't know how to use the app, or online banking. I guess there must have been a way to track this shit pre-internet.

I give the phone back to him. 'I'm so sorry, Baba. I should have checked the text better.'

'It's fine, Ibrahim. Don't worry. This isn't your fault. It's those evil people who made the scam in the first place.' Just hearing him say that spreads some relief through my body.

'Let's hope they get arrested soon,' he continues. 'The fraud man said a lot of elderly people have fallen for it. So I guess it's a bit my fault too.'

'Don't blame yourself,' I tell him, hating that he's feeling as guilty as I am. 'It wasn't your fault either. They make these things to trick people.'

He looks down sadly at his phone, shakes his head a little. 'I just wish . . . I could understand all these things, you know? Just when I think I've got it, something new comes along and I have to learn all about it. This whole internet-banking thing . . . I wish it made more sense to me. I wish I could learn how to use it. Then I wouldn't have to rely on you for it. I wouldn't have to rely on you for so many things. It's just frustrating.'

I'm so shocked I don't know what to reply. Baba is rarely this open about his feelings, even if it's just about being frustrated. He never shows us kids how hard it's been for him. Never once complained about having to live like this. It's why I always felt so guilty about doing the complaining. Like I should be OK with it since he is, since everyone else is. But to know he doesn't like the situation either. To know that he wants to change it too . . . that's incredible. That means there's . . . hope.

'I think . . . I think there are courses you can do, Baba,' I say, remembering what Sura told me earlier. 'To help with things like this. There's things and people to help you. I'll . . . I'll look into it for you and Ma.'

It takes a second for him to nod, reluctantly, but that's still something. Things could . . . actually change. I've been so resigned to the way things are, just accepting it, but now, seeing that even Baba wants change, it makes it seem possible. The thing I didn't even dare dream of. That I could . . . live for myself. That I could live a life where I'm not constantly putting everyone else's needs ahead of mine. Where I'm not permanently anxious about how my parents are doing.

Things could be so much better.

It's truly possible.

22

Sunday night is game night in the Malik house. It all started last year when Mariyam became obsessed with Monopoly and kept begging us to play with her. She'd cry for hours if we said no, so Ma forced us all to play, and it somehow became a weekly thing we all now enjoy. We have a rule that everyone puts their phones face down in the middle of the board. If any of us checks our phone, we have to pay a penalty. I've only been caught out once or twice, but Hamza gets caught every week. Baba's got a pass for this week, considering all the fraud drama. The money still hasn't come back into the account, even though the bank said this morning that it had been sorted. I tried telling Baba about how sometimes it takes a while for information to feed through, and that it's a good thing that the bank sees it as sorted on their end, but he's still attached to his phone, refreshing the app constantly. Hopefully game night will distract him a bit.

'C'mon, Bhaiyya!' Mariyam says. 'If you get a seven, you can take all the money from free parking.'

'Noooo!' Hamza whines, leaning over the Monopoly board. 'That's my money, you can't take it!'

I roll the dice, mumbling an audible prayer about getting a seven. It's nice. This. Being with my family. Being at home and having fun, rather than feeling down and anxious and stressed. Game nights are one of the few times I don't get anxious about being in the house, that I don't worry about being asked to look something up for my parents, or call an electrician or something. The power of board games. Maybe we should get some new games though. Monopoly usually gets . . . heated. And it lasts forever.

The dice land on a four and a two. Hamza gives a whoop.

There's a chirp from the under the pile of Monopoly money in the middle. The sound of a Snapchat message. In the space of a split second, Hamza's hand reaches out and grabs his phone, scattering the paper bills.

'Ha! Fifty-pound penalty!' I say, as Hamza looks at the screen.

Mariyam also yelps with joy and raises a hand for a high five. I give her one, feeling the smile stretch on my face, mirroring hers. Even Baba gives a little laugh.

'Wait, what is this?' Hamza mutters. '"Stand Up, Bridgeport – the finale is here! Which local comedian will win a year-long mentorship with award-winning stand-up guru Kai Matthews and £250?"' he reads out.

Wait, what? I look at Hamza and see that he's picked up my phone, not his, since they look so similar.

'Get off my phone,' I say, yanking it out of his hand. There's adrenaline coursing through me now. My heart's pounding as I turn to see what he's reading. I look at Dexter's message. He's written 'Why are we not screaming about this already?!' over the image of an official poster advertising the competition, featuring all of the contestants' names and the dates of the remaining rounds. My stomach flutters at the sight of my name in big white letters on a poster. Like, a real-life poster. This is going to go up online, and maybe around town. It's as if I'm a real comedian. As if my dream's come true.

The moment is broken by Hamza's snort. Honestly, having siblings is the worst. Especially ones close in age. I look at Hamza, and he's staring at me with a smirk. Shit. He knows. He saw my name there in big white letters.

'Don't read my messages,' I say, hoping to move things along. I push my phone into my pocket, shove it down hard.

'Fifty-pound penalty!' Mariyam squeaks at me excitedly.

I throw a purple note in the middle of the board and push the dice over to Ma, encouraging her to take her turn, trying to move past this moment.

'You're doing . . . stand-up?' Hamza asks, still with a smirk in his voice.

Shit shit shit. He's exposed me now.

Ma looks up at me as she rolls the dice. 'What's "stand-up"?' she asks in Bengali, confused.

'It's when you get on a stage and tell jokes,' Hamza explains before I manage to jump in. 'Ibrahim's entered some joke-telling competition!' He says this quickly with sheer delight in his voice. He knows. He knows Ma and Baba are going to react badly. Going to tell me that this is a waste of time. That I'm going to embarrass them, embarrass our community.

'It's not a joke-telling competition,' I say, more angry than I intended. 'Stand-up isn't just jokes. It's not all about the punchline; it's about creating a relationship with the audience,

133

entertaining them.' I turn to my parents, who've been looking on in confusion, probably unable to fully understand what we're saying.

'It's just something I like doing,' I tell them softly in Bengali. 'I entered a competition. It's like . . . just getting up onstage and . . . talking? I guess. It's hard to explain. You get up and you tell some jokes, sure. But it's more than that. You get to, like, make a difference. Make people laugh, but also think about what you're saying. You get to make people feel less alone. It's . . . I really enjoy it. It makes me happy,'

I wait, almost breathless. I wait for Ma to frown, for her to question what kind of ambition stand-up is. I wait for Baba to tell me that I should be focusing on my studies, not wasting my time when there's no future in comedy as a career.

I've hidden this from my family for years. My passion, my dreams. It was easy to do that when it was just me writing stand-up material in private. This competition . . . it's the first time I've actually *done* anything. It's the first step I've taken towards making this a reality. And it's fucking terrifying to have that shown to my family. It's terrifying having the thing I want most exposed to people who have never seen that side of me.

I'm waiting for them to launch into a rant about how this isn't for people like us, how I should stay within the guidelines of our culture – do something that's 'useful', but instead Ma just nods a little, and looks down at the property cards in her hands. 'That sounds nice,' she says.

Three words.

That's . . . it?

'Nice?' I ask, cautiously. Surely . . . surely she can't be . . .

approving? I've been so sure she'd be against this. Say her signature phrase of 'What will people think?' What will people think of me putting myself up on that stage, exposing myself, our life, our family anecdotes into the world for people to see us, for people to judge us. A tingle runs through my body. I've worried about this moment for so, so long, and it's now unexpectedly . . . over. Done with. But . . . it didn't go in any of the many ways I thought it might.

'It's nice that you have a hobby,' Ma says, still looking down at her cards. 'It's like Hamza and his little football games. Just make sure it doesn't get in the way of your schoolwork.' She leans over to Hamza, shows him a card. 'What does this say?'

'Electricity,' he replies curtly.

Ma repeats the word in broken syllables.

I look to Baba, but he's focused on shaking the dice in his cupped hands. 'If I get a double now, I get out of jail free, right?' he asks Mariyam.

I glare at Hamza. He's always trying to get me in trouble with our parents. But it backfired here, didn't it?

Or did it?

Why do I feel so weird about their response?

I got what I wanted, right? They're not against me doing this. They haven't told me to stop.

My phone pings again. I slip it out of my pocket and look at it under the table. Mariyam is too busy celebrating the fact Baba is still in jail to call penalty, so it's not so risky.

Dexter's sent me another Snap. Now it's a photo of him holding up a massive paper version of the poster. 'Dad printed it out giant. Gonna hang it over my bed!'

I think back to the vision of Dexter and his dad yesterday, their emotional connection. Dexter's dad is always so supportive of anything he does. He even wanted to come along to the competition with us the first week. Dexter was embarrassed and said no, but that he could come if he got into the final. Mr Murgen reluctantly accepted that, but even so, after every stage of the competition he gets Dexter a treat meal and wants a blow-by-blow account of everything that happened.

But of course, that's not how it works with Asian parents. At least not when the dream you want them to support is anything other than being an accountant, lawyer or doctor. I should be used to it by now, surely. And yet the fact we just carry on playing Monopoly and no one even says anything more about this competition, about the fact that it's important enough for them to make posters with my name on, really, really breaks my heart.

23

The nerves have kicked in big time. I barely heard a word any of the teachers said today, which is probably going to be a problem when exams roll around in a few weeks. There's just too much nervousness inside me. Too much adrenaline. The next stage of the comedy competition starts in just three hours. The same amount of time Mr Ferris droned on about atoms today. Normally I'd spend that time going over my set, walking around my room repeating the words under my breath, but of course there's no preparing for being put on the spot tonight. Still, Dexter suggests we go to his after school and practise riffing off each other, throwing each other topic suggestions to help us get used to being under that sudden pressure. He's still hoping we're going to be paired up onstage. I am too, because it's my best shot of rising through the ranks, being with someone I'm used to.

I tell Dexter I need to go home and get changed first, and that I'll meet him at his house. I rush down the street to mine, and open the door to find Mariyam sitting on the stairs, tying the laces on her shoes. She's still in her school uniform and jacket, but she's definitely putting her shoes *on*, rather than taking them off.

'Where are you going?' I ask, confused.

'Doctors',' she says with a grimace.

'What? Why? Are you OK?' I step up to her and press the back of my hand against her forehead. It does nothing, ever, but it's just Asian instinct now, I think, after years of Ma doing the same thing.

'I'm *fine*,' Mariyam grumbles, moving her head away from my touch. 'After I needed the inhaler the other day, Ma made me book an appointment to make sure everything's OK. I told her it was, but she won't believe me.' Mariyam pouts.

I know I should be more worried about her health, but all I can think is that she is *seven* years old, and she's already having to book her own doctor's appointments. There's a sinking feeling in my heart, realising that it's starting for her. She shouldn't even be using the internet except for cute videos and games, and yet she's having to fill in forms to book her own doctor's appointments.

'Come on then, let's go,' Ma says as she rounds the corner, buttoning up a bright pink cardigan over her saree.

'Wait, no,' I say quickly. 'I can take her. They know us now – they're fine with me taking her alone. How come you didn't tell me? I would have come home earlier.' I'm talking too fast, I know, but the idea of Ma taking Mariyam to the doctors' has filled me with panic. She won't be able to explain a thing. What if she says the wrong thing by accident and the doctor gives the wrong medicine or orders the wrong test or something? It's to protect both Mariyam and Ma, really. To save Ma the stress of it all. And I don't want Mariyam to have to feel the pressure of explaining everything herself, of having to fend for herself. She's way too young for that. Plus . . . Ma's bright pink cardigan . . . It's embarrassing.

'You always complain about having to take her,' Ma says, brow furrowed. 'It's fine, I can manage.'

No, you can't, I want to say. I can't say that though. I can't be so rude to her, as true as it is.

'It's just easier if I go,' I tell her instead.

There's a voice inside me that sounds suspiciously like Sura, telling me that it probably would be fine if Ma went. And maybe it would be good for her, forcing her to cope. To adult. To parent. Sura's voice tells me to put myself first. Not to cancel my plans to accommodate my family. That I deserve to be prioritised, that this could be my one thing a day to do for myself.

But she doesn't get it.

She doesn't get the anxiety. She doesn't understand how worried I'd be if Ma went. Doesn't understand that I'd spend the whole time wondering what was happening, whether something bad had happened, and playing out all the different terrible outcomes of this decision.

Anyway, it's not like I can't still go to the competition this evening. I don't need to go to Dexter's first. Sure, he would have been great at calming my nerves about performing, but that's a small price to pay to make sure my family stays safe.

'C'mon, Mariyam, let's go,' I say, holding out my hand before Ma can get even pushier, though I think she's probably secretly grateful.

Thankfully Mariyam's appointment doesn't take long. On the

way home I quiz her on how to use her inhaler, and how to recognise when she needs it, just to make sure.

'I'm *fine*,' she says for the millionth time as we walk up the drive to our front door. 'You're just as bad as Ma.'

'We're just looking out for you,' I say, like the fifty-year-old dad I am on the inside. I put my hand into my trouser pocket for my keys, but they're not there. I check my other pocket. Just my phone. Both my blazer pockets are empty too.

Shit. I must have left my keys on the table when we rushed out earlier.

'You don't by any chance have a house key on you, do you?' I ask Mariyam.

She looks up at me, cocks an eyebrow like the pre-teen she already is on the inside. 'I'm *seven*. I don't know how to use keys.'

Well, shit.

I ring the doorbell and wait for Ma to answer.

A whole minute passes.

'Maybe she's doing a poo,' Mariyam giggles.

I look at my watch. Shit shit shit.

I ring the bell again, over and over and over.

'Stooooooop!' Mariyam whines, covering her ears. 'She probably went for a walk. She was going to go after the doctor's.'

'Ughhhhh. Do you think the back door is open?'

'Maybe,' she replies, igniting some hope in my heart. 'But the gate's always locked so we can't get to it anyway.'

I clench my fists, trying hard not to swear, or scream. This is just typical of my life. My family getting in the way of me doing the one thing I'm passionate about. Of me trying to put myself first for once. See that, Sura? That's what I get for trying to do something just for me.

I take out my phone and press Hamza's number. He *should* be home from school by now, but he always takes forever, going off with his friends to the shops and crap. How come things never go wrong for him when he's selfish like that?

'C'mon, Hamza, pick up, pick up, pick up,' I mutter as the phone rings over and over just like the doorbell.

'He's at football,' Mariyam says, all carefree-like.

Crap. So he is. It's Wednesday after all. I take the phone away from my ear and cut the call that won't get answered. Before I can find another number to call, or google a way to break into your own home, my phone battery dies.

Of course it does.

Mariyam whines as I drag her back towards school. People on the street will probably be calling the police about a suspected kidnapping, or social services about abuse, but I can't think about that now. My head is too full of worries about what will happen if I don't manage to get Hamza's keys. I can't turn up to the competition tonight wearing my uniform. They've probably already written me off because of the panic attacks, and my age. No need to make it worse by turning up in a school shirt with a Coke stain down it. The worries are piling up in my head now, a whirlwind of buzzing.

I need to practise Sura's techniques. The focus-on-the-present stuff. I narrate everything in my head.

I'm going to cross that road, I tell myself. *Then go through the school gates and into the changing rooms. I should be able to find*

141

Hamza's bag and go through it for the keys . . . but what if I go into someone else's bag instead and then a teacher catches me and thinks I'm a thief?

No, no. The literal next step.

Through the gates, up the path, round the corner, to the changing rooms.

I don't know why I expected them to be unlocked.

'Oh for fuck's sake,' slips out of my mouth.

Mariyam gasps. 'You swore! I'm telling Ma!'

'She won't care,' I say, yanking her down the path towards the football field.

I need to find Hamza. I need to get those keys. I can't miss the competition tonight. I just can't. I'm not ready to give up the one thing in life I love. What even am I without stand-up? What other talents do I have? It's not like I'm doing great in school. Always too busy making jokes, laughing with Dexter, to pay attention. If the comedy thing doesn't work out as a career, I don't know what I'm going to do.

'Look!' Mariyam squeals suddenly. 'There's Hamza!'

I pull myself out of my thoughts and realise we're already on the field, all the way up to the pitch, where an actual game is happening, and not just practice, like I had thought. I'm a bit freaked out by the fact I don't remember walking here. That my brain was so loud that I didn't take it in. Anything could have happened to Mariyam and I wouldn't have noticed.

Also, this stupid focus-on-the-next-step advice is bullshit. How the hell am I supposed to focus just on the present when there's *so much* in the future to worry about? It doesn't make sense to just focus on the next step and not plan for the future. Surely the safest thing is to focus on the future and prepare for it?

Stupid Sura and her stupid techniques that don't work. A smatter of applause ripples through the small crowd around us. I notice the spectators are mostly parents. I look onto the pitch and see Hamza running faster than I've ever seen someone run, heading towards the goal. He kicks the ball hard and it flies into the net.

Mariyam lets out a high-pitched screech that makes my ears want to close up. Almost everyone turns to look at her. Even Hamza, who's got the biggest grin on his face. The whistle blows, and the rest of his team runs to embrace Hamza, lifting him up on their shoulders.

God, if he's celebrating, he's going to take ages to go and get changed. To go and get the house keys so we can get back and I can prepare.

Fuck.

24

Hamza takes forever to get back to the changing rooms to grab his stuff. I have to try so hard to not shout at him, because Mariyam's there. But inside I'm exploding. I need to get home. I need to get changed. This whole day has taken so long there's no time for me to prep with Dexter any more. I'm just going to have to go into it blind, and that terrifies me. I really needed that extra time for one of Dexter's hype speeches.

'Where's your trophy then?' Mariyam asks Hamza as we walk (SO FUCKING SLOWLY) back home.

Hamza laughs a little. 'They keep it in school. In a big glass cabinet. I'll show you next time.'

'But *you* scored the goal,' Mariyam says, confused. 'Why does the school get a trophy? The other boys didn't do *anything*. They were just standing around.'

Hamza chuckles again, and it just makes my insides coil up. They're being so fucking slow.

'Gimme your keys,' I say, holding my hand out. 'I'm in a rush, I'll leave the door unlocked for you.'

'What're you in a rush *for?*' Hamza asks.

'Just give me the f—.' I take a breath. 'Just give me the keys,

Hamza. *Please.*' It pains me to even say that word to him, but I'm desperate.

I expect him to make fun of the fact he got me to 'beg', but he just gives me a weird look before handing his keys over.

I take off in a fast walk, leaving them both behind.

Ma's back by the time I rush through the front door, making sure to pick up my keys from the table and replace them with Hamza's. She calls after me as I run up the stairs, asking, 'What took you so long at the doctors'?' I feel a flash of anger flare up in my body, feel the urge to shout at her for leaving the house, for making things worse. But of course I'd never let that emotion show.

I put my phone on charge and shoot Dexter a quick text about all the drama today. He replies with *'Not drama, just excellent material 4 ur next set! Someone deffo thort you were kidnapping Mariyam'* and it's so weird how just that one line from him manages to calm me down.

Maybe *he* should be my therapy. The thing to help my anxiety. Not any of that 'live in the present' bullshit.

My phone's only charged to thirty per cent by the time I have to leave, but it'll have to do. Hopefully there'll be a plug socket at the hall I can steal electricity from. I jog down the stairs and peek my head into the living room.

'I'm . . . going to a friend's house,' I say.

Ma grunts a little as she watches one of her soaps on TV. Baba's just got home from work, so is sitting back in his chair, looking at something on his phone. There's a little sting in

145

my heart. I could tell them. Now that they know about the competition, I could just tell them where I'm going, what I'm off to do, and maybe even tell them how important it is to me, how nervous I am. But . . . I can still remember the way Ma shrugged it off yesterday, when Hamza told her about it. The way Baba didn't even acknowledge it. They don't care.

The guilt though. That never leaves. And as I open the front door, I wonder whether I should sack off the competition and stay home, just in case they need something, in case they need my help. I'm always worried that when I'm onstage, someone will call with an emergency, and I won't be able to come and help. And then whatever bad things happened would be all my fault.

But no! I need to adjust my thinking. That's what Sura's been telling me all along, right? Even if all her techniques don't work, I know I need to do this. This comedy competition is the only thing in my life right now that's just for me. Me doing something I *want* to do, rather than *have* to do. Comedy is my passion. It brings me so much joy. It's wrong to ignore that. There's no *need* for me to ignore that. I can do both. I can look after the family without making myself miserable. It's possible, I'm sure it is.

Dexter's dad opens the door to me. When he sees it's me, he puts his hands on his hips and sticks his chest out – superhero-style. He's wearing a white T-shirt, with a photo of Dexter as a little kid printed on it, sticking his tongue out and pulling a face, with a pair of underpants on his head.

'How much do you think he'll hate it?' Mr Murgen asks me.

146

A huge grin spreads across my face. 'Oh my God, SO much. Like, more than he hates white chocolate.'

'Perfect!' Mr Murgen grins even wider than me, then closes his jacket over the T-shirt. 'I'm gonna bust it out just as he gets into his performance tonight.'

'He's letting you come?' I ask, shocked, as I walk through to the living room.

'Only because he bribed me!' Dexter says, appearing behind me. I turn to look at him and immediately feel awkward. He's standing in the exact same spot he was when I saw him in the vision with Sura the other day, and it all comes back to me in a flash. Him crying with his dad. He doesn't know I know, obviously, but I'm reminded about how I've seen him at his lowest point, and the worst thing is that I don't think he would have ever *wanted* me to see him like that.

'Isn't it worse to be a brib*ee* than a brib*er*?' Mr Murgen asks Dexter, still smirking. They get into a joke argument, and I'm a bit stunned. I thought things here would be super awkward, but Dexter seems . . . happy. Like, *genuinely* happy. There's a change in Mr Murgen too. The ease with which he teases Dexter – he's not walking on eggshells any more. It really does seem like that night has changed things for both of them. Maybe . . . maybe I did make some kind of difference? Like, in the tiniest, minuscule way.

'Right, boys, get your shoes on,' Mr Murgen says. 'Let's get this show on the road!'

'Dad, you're the only one *not* wearing shoes . . .' Dexter says with a chuckle.

Mr Murgen looks down at his feet and jolts in shock, as if his shoes just suddenly disappeared. He gasps dramatically. 'So

I am,' he says. He looks up at Dexter and says, 'BRB,' before walking off towards the stairs.

Dexter groans loudly. 'You CANNOT be embarrassing me like that at the show!' he shouts after his dad.

I can't help but laugh, imagining how Dexter's going to react when his dad unveils the custom T-shirt.

'OK, I'm too curious, you gotta tell me what he bribed you –' My voice just cuts out when I notice the photo on the wall. It's the picture of Mrs Murgen – the one I dropped the other day, but it's been reframed, and hung up above the fireplace. Now that I look around, I see there are more photos of her up on the walls. Sort of like how it was before she died.

Dexter notices me looking at a picture resting on the sideboard and walks over to it. He reaches out with just a finger and nudges it the tiniest bit, so that it's perfectly straight. I catch the soft smile on his face.

'She's finally escaped her cupboard coffin,' Dexter says, referring back to my joke from the other day.

I can't help but smile too. 'So she's a zombie now, then?' I ask.

'Yep,' Dexter replies. 'And she's in every room of the house.'

'Even in the toilet?' I ask.

'Even in the toilet,' Dexter confirms.

'Remind me never to pee in your house again,' I laugh.

The scoreboard is standing tall and proud in the reception area of the community centre once again. But this time there's no crowd around it. Dexter stops at the door, and I notice him fiddling with his hands, trying to pull his fingers out of their sockets by the looks of it.

'You OK, mate?' I ask, concerned he's in pain or something.

He turns to look at me, and I spot the nervousness on his face in the split second before he plasters on an over-the-top grin. It's literally like he's switched from zero to one hundred.

'I'm awesome,' Dexter replies, grin somehow widening. 'Just hoping they don't base my points on how embarrassing my dad is gonna be tonight. Even though I told him to pretend we don't know each other, I just know he's gonna do something peak Dad.' For the first time I realise he's covering up his nerves with humour. He should be able to talk to me about these things. I mean, we've been best friends for seven years now.

But then . . . I haven't told him about my panic attacks. I don't think I ever could. It's just not how our friendship is. We're guys. We don't talk about the deep stuff. Like what my home is like – how my parents can't function without me doing everything for them. We don't talk about how my brain is always buzzing with worry, with panic. And we definitely don't talk about how I've started seeing Sura.

But we should be able to. We should be able to confide in each other. After all, what are best friends for? Maybe I'm the one who needs to try a bit harder.

'C'mon, let's go see how far up you've gone,' I say, pushing him towards the board. I need to be his hype man. I need to instil the same confidence in him that he does in me when I'm having a wobble. The same confidence *I* have in *him*. 'You're gonna smash this, you know you are,' I tell him. 'You and me at the Apollo, yeah?'

'We gotta get through this first,' he reminds me. 'There's just . . . so much pressure tonight, innit?' he says in a quiet voice. 'I mean, not just because Dad's here. It's . . . almost over. They're making cuts tonight. Top three only going through to the finals. It's . . . there's some really talented people competing.'

I'm legit a bit shocked that he's actually admitting he's scared, rather than making a joke of it. And to be fair, my instinctive reaction is to make a joke about me being the other talented people competing. But the only way things are going to change for the better between us is if I start to change the way I am with him, isn't it? If he's feeling brave enough to be open about his worries, I should take a step towards him too.

'Yeah, and you're one of them,' I tell him. 'You're *so* talented, dude. And that's not just me saying that as your best friend. You've been in the top four the whole time. I know you'll be fine. And yes, even though tonight is different, it's literally what you do every day. You improv your whole life, mate. Every single thing someone says, you know how to crack the best joke after it. Even now, when I finish this mushy-ass speech, you're going to make the best joke. And that's how I know you're going to be safe.'

There's a flash of a sentimental proper smile in him, before he transforms it into a cheeky one.

'So I'm taking that super mushy-ass speech to mean you will give me your place if you get to the final and I don't,' he says.

I roll my eyes and shove him towards the board again. 'What did I say?'

When I look at the scoreboard, I instinctively go looking for Dexter at the top, obvs, because he's bound to be up there.

And up there he is.

'WHAT did I tell you, eh?' I say, wrapping my arm around his neck and pulling him in to me. I expect him to be smiling to see he's still in second place, but again, there's just worry on his face. Seriously, since when did we swap roles?

'What's wrong?' I ask, letting him go.

He turns to me, his eyes widening as if I've never asked him that question before. He looks away, cracking his knuckles.

'Nothing,' he replies. 'It's great. Second the best, right?'

'You're only a point away,' I say, realising Dexter's determined to get to the top. Maybe he feels the need to prove himself. 'You've got this,' I tell him. 'If you want, I'll heckle the guy who's top when he's on. Ooh, I can totally sabotage him if we're paired up together. I'll just start naming fish.'

This makes Dexter laugh. A genuine laugh.

'Seriously, mate, you'll be fine,' I say, trying to put into my tone that I really truly believe that, and he should too.

'Thanks, mate,' he says. 'You're doing pretty fine yourself, eh? We might get that shot of doing the finals together after all.'

I look back at the board, starting from the bottom, but I find my name way up high. Just two below Dexter. Only a few points between us.

'How the hell am I fourth?' I say without really meaning to.

'Probably that bit about rubber ducks you did last time. That was a good one.'

Wow. I'm actually . . . I'm doing well. I'm so close to the top three. So close to being included in the final. If I do well today . . . it could happen. I came into this thinking I wasn't good enough, and most of me still really does believe that. But I guess this is like that thing Sura keeps telling me to do, innit? Look at the facts, Ibrahim. And the facts are right there on the scoreboard.

More people start coming into the reception area, trying to nudge forward and see the scores. Dexter and I go into the main hall. He goes for drinks while I save our usual table, all the while fizzing with the excitement of being fourth. Of being so, so close. I give a nod to Mr Murgen, who's sitting conspicuously alone a few tables over. He gives me a grin and flashes his shirt at me again.

'We gotta do a toast, man,' Dexter says, sitting down with our lemonades, thankfully with his back to his dad.

'A toast?' I ask. 'What are we, thirty?' I go to grab my drink from the table, but he pushes it away from me.

'C'mon, man, this is a big night. The penultimate round. Make or break. We've come this far. We should celebrate.'

'Since when were you such a sappy git?' I say. It's instinctive, and slips out, but I can see Dexter's face fall a tiny bit. God, I really need to practise this sensitivity stuff.

'How about we save the speeches for next week, when we're both definitely, *definitely* in the final?' I ask, trying to move past the moment, trying not to let Dexter feel the way I do when I say something I feel is stupid because of how everyone else reacts.

'Sounds like a plan,' Dexter says, smiling. He clinks his glass with mine and we both take a big sip of our drinks.

25

'Oh my God, you two are *so* good together,' Sophie Hart says as she, Dexter and I come off stage to huge applause.

'And you!' I say, unable to keep the smile off my face or the grin out of my voice. I push my glasses up my sweaty nose before wiping my forehead with the back of my hand.

'For real, Sophie,' Dexter adds as we huddle off to the side. He's also grinning so hard. 'You were amazing. We make an amazing team.'

'Right?!' she squeaks. 'I thought I might be third-wheeling when they called you two up together, but I think we were the perfect group, right?'

We're all on such a performance high. I've been ecstatic ever since the judges called Dexter's name right after mine to work together. And if I had to choose anyone from the other bunch of contestants, Sophie would *so* be the one. We all have our own specialist topics – Dexter with his dead mum, me with being a brown guy in a white town, and Sophie with her mental-health stuff. They may seem miles apart, but weirdly they worked super well together. I even did a bit about mental health in the Asian community, and how there's no word for depression in Bengali. I had a minuscule panic, thinking maybe Dexter could see through it, see that it wasn't a bit but my reality. I think maybe a part of me hoped he *would* see through it. That way he could know without me having to actually talk about it.

But he didn't. Of course.

'There's no way we ain't coming tops,' Dexter says, grin still spread all over his face.

He might be right. We were the second group up, so we got to see the first three do their set. They were . . . a bit awkward, to say the least. It's why I was even more terrified. I think we might . . . actually do well, points wise. I'm so lucky to have been paired with these two. They're already doing so well, and now they're going to pull me up with them. Maybe . . . there's even a chance of making it to the finals? Me, Dexter and Sophie would be the best line up for the end. My stomach starts getting butterflies at the thought. That *I* could be in the finals. That I could . . . maybe win?

'You two *have* to come to stand-up night at my uni,' Sophie says, getting out her phone. 'Gimme your numbers, I'll text you the deets. You two would be perf.'

Sophie tells us all about her friends at university, and how they have monthly open-mic stand-up nights, and once again the butterflies are back, just at the thought of being in an atmosphere like that. Of being around other people interested in stand-up. People who are *good* at stand-up. It's been amazing having Dexter, but if we could build a wider network of comedy friends, it would be such a good way of trying out material and hearing about other events and competitions. The perfect way to work our way up to the Apollo.

* * *

Dexter goes over to talk to his dad during the break, even though he said he was going to pretend that table was empty all night. I don't make fun of him. Instead I watch as Mr Murgen shows Dexter his T-shirt and Dexter doubles over laughing. I see the smile bloom on Dexter's face as his dad hugs him tight. I decide to let them have their moment, turning back to Sophie and asking her more about her stand-up nights at uni.

Sophie stays at our table to watch the last group of contestants, who get given the scenario of being in a bank when a robber comes in. She fits right in with me and Dexter. She's one of those people who you don't feel self-conscious around. There's no worrying in my head about whether she hates me, because she's emitting such a positive vibe. She hasn't stopped smiling all night. She seems like one of those people who's always happy. And that transfers outwards, I think. I'm in a great mood. And it's because I'm doing something I love. Something just for me. Just like Sura said.

I look to the back of the room, at the noticeboard with the poster for the missing cat who looks possessed. The spot where Sura and I once stood watching the past version of myself have a panic attack onstage. A part of me expects her to be there, watching, smiling at me, like the mysterious spiritual guides in cheesy Hollywood films. But of course she's not there. I've realised now that there are rules to her existence. And one of those rules is that she only exists in that little back room, unless she's with me in a vision of the past or present.

I should go see her. I bet she'd be happy to know how well tonight went. A lot of it is down to her and how much she's helped me, for sure. Plus I didn't really properly thank her for the other day, when I broke in. I was in such a dark place and she managed to pull me out. She saved me.

'Just going to the loo,' I say as I get off my chair. I slink off down the side and into the corridor. I feel like anything related to Sura needs to be done sneakily, even though no one here is probably paying any attention to me. Too busy listening to Marshal Erick boring the robber to death with his list of fish names.

I walk down the corridor, checking over my shoulder every few seconds, preparing the defence that I got lost looking for the clearly marked toilets. Just in case. I press down the door handle and push the door open, still feeling good, on a high. Sura's going to be so excited about how well things are going.

But . . . when I get into the room, she's not there.

I turn the lights on and look in the corner behind the door. But she's nowhere to be seen.

'Sura?' I whisper.

No response.

'Hello?' I say a bit louder, just in case she's . . . sleeping? Or something.

But still nothing.

Where is she? She said she would always be here for me when I needed her. Maybe that's the point. She's only ever appeared when I was having a panic attack, or in a bad place. Maybe she only appears when I 'need' her to help me through a dark thing, a dark time. Should I try and bring on a panic attack just to see her? No, that's stupid, right? I should just be grateful that I'm feeling good right now, that I don't *need* her.

156

But wait . . . does this mean . . . I'll *never* see Sura again? I didn't even get to say goodbye, or thank her properly, tell her how much she's helped me, how much I appreciate her. I didn't get to say any of that to her. If I had known last time was the last time I'd see her, I would have done so much differently . . .

I close my eyes tight, think of Sura, try and manifest her. I think of the way she smiles at me, even when I'm being a dick to her, the way she encourages me, the way she makes me feel like I'm not completely unfixable. I need her in my life. I do.

I open my eyes, expecting her to be standing in front of me. Blue scarf as neat and pretty as always.

'Hey, Ibrahim,' she'd say when she saw me. In the same tone she always says it in.

But she's not there. The room is still empty. And feels so much smaller now, without her in it.

There's nothing else to do. No other way I can think of making her come here, making her appear.

With a heavy heart I take one last look at the room, turn the lights off and go back to the main hall, to Dexter and Sophie.

26

My good mood from the competition lasts all week. Sure, there's a lingering anxiety about whether I did enough to get in the top three, to make it to the finals. But it's not pressing on my mind all the time. I'm able to enjoy other things, without the stress consuming me, which is new.

I've been so focused on the competition I've been slacking on school stuff. I know I should just hole up in my room and do some homework or revision, but today I feel like I want to spend some time with my family instead. It's weird – I'm so used to avoiding my family as much as possible, trying to avoid any sudden 'can you do this for me?'s. But . . . today I feel like I need to just do something fun with my family. You get back what you put into the world, right?

God, that sounds like something Sura would say. Maybe now that she's not going to be around any more, my brain is filling in the things she would have said to me.

I'm realising now that even though I do things for my parents, for my family, it's mostly only functional things. Like, I only help them to get things done, to move things along. It's transactional almost. There's no emotion behind it. Well, except guilt and anxiety and panic, I guess. I need to show them that I can be there as a loving, caring person too. A son who helps his parents not out of duty, but out of love.

I can do that. I need to do that.

I go into the kitchen, where Ma is cooking, and ask if I can do anything to help. Not surprisingly, she turns to me and gives me a look, like I've just asked her where babies come from.

'I just thought you might like some help,' I explain with a shrug. 'You're always cooking alone, feeding all five of us; it must be a lot of work.'

I see a slight smile appear on her face. It's not often I make her smile. This is definitely something I should keep up.

'Fine, then,' Ma says, not letting on how pleased she is, which is typical of her – it seems to be an Asian-parent thing where you can't show your emotions to others.

Not *just* a parent thing, I guess.

'You can peel those potatoes,' she says, nodding to the bag on the counter. 'I'm making aloo baazi, your favourite.'

I get straight to it, peeling as carefully as I can, making sure not to leave even a tiny bit of skin on. It takes a while, but I'm pleased with myself, pleased I've managed to do something to help, something that's fiddly and boring. I saved her from having to do that.

'What?!' she squeals when she comes over to my counter. 'You peeled the whole bag?'

I turn to her. 'You told me to!'

'Not *all* of them! What am I going to do with so many potatoes? I only need five.'

'How was I supposed to know?' I ask. 'You just said to peel those potatoes!'

'Ugh, you should use your common sense,' she says, coming over and yanking the peeler out of my hand.

She's angry. I made her angry. Upset. I made things worse. She was fine on her own, and I just came and ruined her mood.

'Sorry, Ma,' I say. I go to run a hand through my hair, but then remember my fingers are covered in potato juice. 'Can't you freeze the rest of them so they don't go to waste?'

She tuts as she puts some of the peeled potatoes into a bowl of water. 'You can't *freeze* potatoes. I'm just going to have to cook something else now.'

Oh God. I came in to help her with her workload and I've done the exact opposite. That's how useless I am.

'Sorry,' I repeat lamely.

'Just go and look after Mariyam. I don't need help.' Her voice has returned to normal, no more anger in it, but I still feel like shit. I couldn't even help her with something as simple as peeling potatoes.

'Are you sure I can't do anything else?' I ask. 'I'll pay more attention.'

'No, it's OK. You go do your homework. Oh God, something's burning.' She rushes back over to the stove to stir a pan. The bitter smell of burnt spices fills the air.

I could ask her again, but she would probably get annoyed. Best to leave her to it. I'll think of another way to do something nice for her. Maybe I could order her some flowers. I'd probably mess that up too. Probably end up getting her flowers she's allergic to or something.

160

I go into the living room, looking for Baba, trying to think of a way I could do something nice for him without it seeming like a chore. But he's not there. Just Mariyam, laying sprawled on the floor, watching TV.

'Whatcha watching?' I ask from the doorway.

'Shhhhh,' she hisses angrily, eyes not moving from the screen.

God, I can't even make my little sister happy. And she's usually over the moon with just a high five. Maybe I should give up?

But no. I refuse. It would be so easy to go back to that life of being miserable. But like Sura would say, the only way to change things is to make an effort. And the most important thing to have is the desire for change, and man, do I have that. I want things to change so bad. I *need* things to change in my life. I can't keep having panic attacks, feeling like everything is about to come crashing down. No. This week I've tasted what it's like to feel good. I've not had a single panic attack, or even a bad day. And it's been great. Maybe the trick is to go back to what Sura's said to me in the past.

I think back and remember the night we went to Dexter's house, when she said it's not always the biggest things or actions that make a difference. Sometimes it can be something tiny.

I go over to Mariyam and sit down cross-legged next to her, leaning back against the sofa. She might not want me to speak to her, but I can just sit with her. Be with her. That means something.

I start to get into the cartoon she's watching – something about genies and wishes and gems.

'So that tall one wants to steal all the gems?' I ask Mariyam.

'Yeah!' she replies enthusiastically. 'Zeta always wants to steal the gems from Shimmer and Shine. She's the baddie.'

'Is her baby dragon bad too?'

'Noooo! Nazboo is so cute.'

We watch the rest of the episode together, and Mariyam even tells me what's going to happen next. It's clear she's watched this episode many times before. Baba walks into the living room as the next episode starts up. Normally he tells Mariyam to turn her cartoons off and give him the remote, but today he just goes and sits down in his chair.

I thought he would be back to normal once the money returned to his account after the whole scam-text thing, but it's been days, and still he seems sad and stressed. Maybe something else is bugging him. Maybe he has something else going on in his life and is hiding it, the way I hide my panic attacks. God, why hadn't I thought of that before?

I look at his face as he sits in his armchair and stares blankly at the TV. He looks . . . fed up. Bored. Sad.

'Are you OK, Baba?' I ask, trying to make the effort.

He looks at me, head on his hand. He gives me a weird look. I don't blame him. I've never asked him how he is before. It's not something we do in this family, talk about feelings or emotions with each other. So I try harder.

'Are you doing anything today?' I ask. It's his day off, and now that I think about it, he never does anything on his days off. Unless Ma needs to do something, or he has something in the house to take care of. He never does anything just for himself. He never goes out with friends. Does he even have any friends, other than the people who work at the restaurant

162

with him? I wonder if there's anything in his life he's passionate about, anything he wants to do. If there's anything he loves as much as I love stand-up. But I realise I don't know anything about him. I guess we barely spend any time together, other than game night, when we only talk about the game. Maybe he'd like to join a club that plays games? Is there even such a thing for adults?

I get out my phone and start googling things for adults in our area. I feel a blush rise up my cheeks as the top suggestions are X-rated. I angle my screen so that Baba and Mariyam can't see and reword my search. Things start to look a bit more promising. There are clubs for things like bowls, gardening, chess. But I don't know if Baba likes any of those things. And anyway, I doubt he'd enjoy going to socialise with a bunch of old white men who probably think he doesn't belong in this country.

I change my search again, looking to see if there's anything for Asian people specifically. My heart skips a beat when one of the suggestions is a social group for Bengali men. Could this *be* any more perfect? It's not a specific activity, it seems. Just Bengali men sitting together, drinking tea. That sounds PERFECT. He could make some friends, have someone to talk to about back home and the good old days. I think Baba needs an outlet. Something that brings him joy, like comedy brings me joy and fulfilment. Maybe this group could be a way to him finding that.

'Baba, what are you doing later?' I ask. 'I found something you might like.'

He actually lowers his hand and looks at me this time.

163

27

Tomorrow's the night. The final of the stand-up competition. The night I find out whether I've got what it takes to actually have a chance of becoming a comedian, of making my dream a reality one day. The organisers are going to announce the three people with the highest points at the start, so we won't know until literally minutes before if we're performing. My brain has been going into overdrive worrying about it, but it's quite exciting too. I wasn't far below Nick Miller, who was third last time, so there's technically a chance of me being a finalist.

I am nervous as fuck.

Dexter and I are in his room, preparing sets for the final, just in case we get picked. Well, we both know Dexter's going to get picked (even though he pretends there's a chance he might not).

'I think I need to change things up,' he says, popping a peanut M&M (the snack he says gives him all his good ideas) in his mouth and crunching loudly.

'Yeah, good idea,' I reply. 'Everyone knows Skittles are better than M&Ms,'

'Blasphemy!' Dexter says, throwing an M&M at me. I expertly dodge it.

'Throwing haram food at a Muslim can be considered a hate crime, y'know.'

'You're a hate crime,' he replies, crunching another M&M. 'Anyway, I wasn't talking about snacks, I was talking about my set. Do you think the dead-mum stuff is getting boring?'

'What? No way. You always keep it fresh. Everyone loves it.'

'Hmm, maybe,' he mutters.

'But . . . maybe you could expand on it a bit?' I suggest, thinking about how I've been considering doing the same with my sets. Sophie Hart has really inspired me with the way she can joke about her mental health, but in a way where it doesn't make it less real, or less horrible. I also think things need to be said about the lack of mental-health awareness in the Asian community, and maybe my comedy can eventually help other people open those conversations, the way Sura helped me talk about my problems. Obviously I'd have to widen my audience first.

'Expand how?' Dexter asks. 'Like, go into detail about how she died? The gasping? The way she probably clutched her chest like in those films? How sick are you, mate?' he jokes.

'Don't forget about her dinner that got left untouched,' I add.

He laughs and throws another M&M at me.

'No, I meant, like . . .' I push my glasses up my nose, thinking about the scene Sura showed me between Dexter and his dad.

'Like, just . . . grief in general, maybe? How hard it's been,

I mean . . . how hard it *can* be . . . The way no one really talks about people after they're gone . . . or . . . something like that maybe? I dunno.' I turn back to my screen, scroll down the near-empty document waiting for Dexter to say how weird I'm being, that I've made a stupid suggestion.

'Hmm,' he says instead. He goes from laying on his stomach to sitting cross-legged like me. 'That . . . might actually be a good idea.'

A spark of joy lights up within me. A compliment from Dexter is worth a lot. I smile as he starts tapping away on his laptop. You know Dexter's churning out gold when he's absolutely silent.

Now that I know he's concentrating, I start my own research for my new set. I think back to my appointment with Dr Stenhouse way back when, the symptoms she went through, the ones she said might mean I have an anxiety disorder, that I might be depressed. I had shrugged it all off back then, desperate not to be labelled 'crazy' or 'mentally ill', but the more I look at the information available about these things, the more I relate. The websites talk about how sometimes mental illness comes from the way brains are wired, like something unavoidable, and sometimes it's linked to circumstances. There's no denying that with the way my life is, having to deal with so many things for my parents, having that extra pressure of being responsible for stuff beyond my age . . . it's no wonder, right? I think that's what Sura said one day anyway. It makes *sense* for me to struggle with my mental health.

I'm on the second page of my Google search about mental illness when I spot something that both shocks and confuses me. A blog post entitled 'My Mental Health Journey' by . . . Imran Mahmood, one of my favourite stand-up comedians, and one who happens to be both Muslim and Bengali. I had completely forgotten about him! I used to watch his clips every day, but then he suddenly stopped doing sets and stopped posting skits on his socials. There was a rumour going around online that he was dead.

But no, this blog is dated just last week. My heart starts pounding as I read his words, read about how he had to take a break from social media and comedy and even his day job because of his mental health. Because he was having almost daily panic attacks and became agoraphobic. He talks about the stigma of mental illness among men, especially in the Asian community. He talks about why it took him so long to get help. And every single word of it resonates with me.

Imran talks about being officially diagnosed with depression and generalised anxiety disorder, and how he realised that it's not something to be ashamed of. That asking for help isn't anything to be ashamed of.

'If you had a broken leg, you wouldn't be ashamed of getting help for that, so why is mental health any different?'

It makes so much sense, and deep down I think I always knew that this was my truth. That there was something going on with my brain. Imran goes on to say how asking for help was the best thing he did. That alongside medication, he started a CBT course that helped him manage his thoughts. He talks about it a bit, and I realise it's like what Sura's been teaching me these past few weeks. And I know for sure that her stuff has helped a lot. So maybe . . . maybe getting more help is the answer?

I still don't think a therapist is for me. I don't want to sit down with a stranger and pour my heart out, always wondering if they're secretly judging me, making fun of me. But maybe . . . maybe the sorts of things that Sura has been teaching me, learning how to manage my thoughts, maybe more of that could help.

I do this thing sometimes when I make a deal with myself. For example, if I do twenty minutes of revision, I can have a doughnut. Like a motivational tool. So I make a deal with myself. If I manage to be one of the three people chosen as a finalist, then I'll do it. I'll get help. I'll make an appointment to talk to Dr Stenhouse about all of this.

But first, the competition.

28

I have to leave in an hour to meet Dexter and I still haven't decided what to wear. I try on outfit after outfit to get that perfect balance of cool and casual. But also semi-professional. I need to make sure I don't look like a stupid kid trying to go above my level. A part of my brain thinks that if I dress well, maybe they're more likely to pick me as a finalist, which is stupid, obviously, but my brain is used to thinking up all the wildest possibilities. I get so desperate that I sneak into Hamza's room to look for something. Everything in my wardrobe just seems lame. Hamza at least gives off an air of cool, even though he's an idiot sometimes. And we're about the same size. Though I am of course taller. There was a dark green hoodie he wore the other week that I remember secretly wanting. I make sure he's occupied with the TV downstairs and sneak it out. I'll have to take it in my backpack so he doesn't see me wearing it though.

I know I should probably go over my prepared set, run through it again to make sure it's locked in my head. But I'm worried that if I try and do any more work on it that it'll get all muddled in my brain. It's like when you're just about to go and do an exam. So many people say that cramming last minute doesn't help at all. And plus I really think I've gotten much better at stand-up through this competition. Like, I haven't just been showing off my skills, but learning new ones. Like getting over my fear of improv.

I shove Hamza's hoodie into my backpack and start trying to fix my hair.

'Ibrahim!' Ma calls up the stairs. 'Are you ready?'

'Ready . . . for what?' I ask back, tentatively. She can't be talking about the competition, right? I know Hamza outed me at game night the other night, but she seemed so uninterested. There's no way she knows tonight's the final. Unless . . . unless she's actually taking an interest? Maybe she got Hamza to look it up so she could support me. I spent years wanting my family to pay attention to my interests, my hobbies, my passions. Could it be? Could it finally be happening?

'Ready for Radiya's house!' Ma calls up, impatient. 'Hurry up!'

Wait . . . what? We didn't have any plans to go anywhere today. I remember being so relieved seeing that the date for the final didn't clash with one of Ma's random outings.

She likes to go over to Auntie Radiya's house regularly, but I would have remembered, for sure, if she had planned for us all to go today.

'Ibrahim, come on!' Baba shouts now. God, if Baba's in on it too, this is a proper visit.

I come out of my room, onto the landing, and shout down, 'Why are we going to Auntie Radiya's?'

Of course no one answers, even though I'm closer and

therefore louder than I was in my room. I huff and go downstairs, find Ma in the kitchen and repeat the question.

'She bought a new bed, and I said you and Hamza would build it for her. She and your uncle are too old to do these things now,' she says, as she fills a yellow-stained Tupperware container with her home-grown chillies. 'Get your shoes on.'

'I . . . I have stuff to do,' I say. I should tell her it's the final of the competition today, but some part of me can't handle her disinterest in it.

'I already told Radiya you'd do it,' she replies, not even looking at me.

'Can't we do it tomorrow?' I ask, trying to think of an excuse that'll get them to leave me here. 'I have homework.'

'You should've done your homework earlier,' Ma tuts. 'But you can do it when you come back. Now hurry up.' She puts the tub of chillies into a bag filled with other containers and leaves the room.

I follow her. 'Ma, I really . . . I really need to get this done tonight. Can't we just go another night? I can build the bed myself, just . . . tomorrow instead.'

'Ibrahim, the poor woman's been sleeping on a broken bed for months. You're two young, fit boys; you should do this for her. I've already had Hamza moaning at me. You're the older brother. You should be setting an example.'

As if on cue, Hamza trudges down the stairs. His expression probably matches mine. Our eyes meet and he rolls his eyes in a rare sign of solidarity.

'Ibrahim, why aren't you ready yet?' Baba asks as he walks into the kitchen. 'They're waiting for us.'

And so that's that. I guess I'm going to Auntie Radiya's house.

I check my watch discreetly as I tie up my laces, with the entire family watching me, waiting for me. I'm panicking (not panic-attack style, just general panic). I need to think of a way out of this. Could I just say I'll walk instead and meet them there? And then run away? No, of course I could never do that.

Maybe I can ask Hamza to build the bed himself so I can leave? Or we could do it super quickly and then leave? There might be enough time.

Normally I'd just accept the loss, accept that I'm powerless against my parents' wishes. But not tonight. Tonight is special. It's about stand-up. It's the last stage! This is my best chance. There's no way I can let this opportunity pass. I would hate myself if I didn't fight for this. If I can't fight for it now, I'll never be able to.

I have to find a way to get to the final.

I just have to.

29

I form a plan on the drive over. I sow some seeds of me not feeling well. Slight groaning and tummy holding. I'm going to sneak out when it's time and . . . deal with the consequences later.

OK, fine, it's a terrible plan. But it's all I've got.

I text Dexter – *'Roadblock with family plans. Meet u there. Use ur most excellent improv skills n stall everything if I'm late.'*

He texts back almost immediately – *'ooh sounds mysterious. I am up 4 the challenge. I'll get Dad 2 fake a heart attack or something. We can say it runs in the family.'*

Ma and Baba plop themselves down on the sofa as soon as we arrive. Auntie Radiya goes to make tea and snacks. No one mentions the bed that so desperately needs to be built. Even Hamza doesn't seem to care. He just sits on the sofa, tapping away on his phone.

'Hamza, c'mon,' I say after a while. 'Let's go upstairs.'

He cocks an eyebrow at me questioningly.

'To build the bed? Literally the whole reason we came?' I turn to Uncle Mustafa. 'Is everything up there?'

'Yes, yes,' he replies, flapping his hand at me for interrupting the super-important conversation he and Baba are having about the weather back home in Bangladesh.

I leave the room and rush up the stairs, not caring if Hamza follows me or not. I'll build this damn bed alone if I have to.

The bed turns out to be a much simpler model than I was expecting, which fills me with relief. It looks like we just have to make a simple frame, and the slats are already put together, so they just need to be rolled out. We could have this finished in time for me to go and meet Dexter. Still haven't figured out exactly *how* I'm going to leave, but . . . one thing at a time.

'Why are you in such a rush?' Hamza huffs after I tell him to screw faster for the third time.

'I just . . . I want to get this over and done with,' I reply, sneakily checking the time on my phone.

'Imagine if you don't tighten something enough and the bed breaks when they're sleeping,' Hamza says with a snort.

'I'm so glad you said sleeping, and not something else,' I say, unable to stop the joke.

Hamza exclaims in disgust. 'Oh God, gross!'

I feel a little blush rise up, realising I probably shouldn't be making such jokes around my younger brother.

'Should we play a prank on them?' I ask quickly, trying to change the subject. 'Like, um, I dunno . . . we could . . . put a whoopee cushion inside the mattress?' I cringe at the suggestion, at how lame it must sound to him, but I'm babbling, trying to get past the awkwardness.

Hamza laughs a little. 'Uncle Mustafa doesn't need one. He already farts enough!'

Suddenly there's a crash behind us – Hamza and I both jump and turn to find Mariyam buried underneath the huge mattress wrapped in plastic, that was leaning against the wall a second ago.

'Oops,' she says, followed by a giggle.

'Ugh, Mariyam!' I shout, walking over to free her. 'I told you to stop messing about.'

'But I'm *boooored*,' she whines as she stands up and brushes herself off.

'Go downstairs then. We're almost done.'

'Er, no, we're not,' Hamza says, picking up a large bag of unopened screws.

I check the time on my phone again.

Shit.

When we're FINALLY done with the bed (it turned out each slat needed attaching at both ends), I race down the stairs, even though I'm already sweaty AF from the work. Hopefully Dexter will have some deodorant with him at the centre.

'Bed's done,' I tell everyone in the living room.

No one says anything in response. Uncle Mustafa just looks at me and nods. The Asian-uncle way of saying 'thank you'.

'So, um . . .' I say awkwardly, 'can we go home now?' I ask as Mariyam and Hamza come in and settle down on the sofa.

There's still just about enough time to make it to the competition, but that relies on my parents doing things quickly, and judging by how many samosas are left on their plates, I don't think they'll be ready to go any time soon.

'We're talking,' Baba says, a smidge angrily.

This is normally when I'd shut up. Just accept the loss and sit down. But not tonight.

'It's fine, I can . . . I can walk home alone,' I say.

'We'll leave soon, just sit down,' Ma says, also sounding irritated.

'Eat some samosas,' Auntie Radiya says, pushing the plate towards Mariyam. 'They're vegetable.'

Mariyam scrunches up her nose.

'I just . . . I'm not feeling well,' I say, pressing a hand to my stomach. 'I think I need to go to bed. Or maybe just . . . out to get some air? The walk back should be –'

'Be quiet and sit down,' Ma orders. The look on her face is one that I can't argue with.

I sit on the sofa next to Mariyam, bouncing my knee, watching the clock on the wall, waiting for Baba to slap his palms on his thighs and say, 'Right then,' before standing up to leave.

Five minutes pass.

Mariyam whines so much I let her watch me play a game on my phone, hoping that'll be a good distraction.

It's not.

Another ten minutes pass and they're all still yapping away happily. Auntie Radiya's only daughter is away at university, so it's just them in the house. I guess they get bored and love having my parents – and sometimes us kids too – over.

Auntie Radiya gets up off the sofa and my heart starts racing, thinking she might be the one to end this night, FINALLY. I prepare to jump up off the sofa, get my shoes on, waiting for Baba to start the car.

But instead, Auntie Radiya just asks 'Another cup of tea?'

* * *

There's only half an hour till the show starts. My parents are on their third cup of tea. It's getting too late. I have to leave soon if I want any chance of making it. Of having a chance at the competition. The only thing left is to sneak out. I've already seeded the thing about not feeling well, so hopefully when I leave the room they'll think I'm just in the toilet. Maybe I should sneak out of the bathroom window, leave the door locked for added authenticity.

I don't think about how I'll sneak back in here after the event, whether I'll even get a chance to, or if my family will realise I'm missing before then. I don't think about anything other than getting to the community centre.

My heart's pounding away like crazy, and I feel like everyone can hear it, like they'll figure me out and catch me in the act. But then maybe the pounding heart can be one of my symptoms to make this sickness more believable. I close the game I was playing with Mariyam, and she whines a little.

'I'm just . . . going to the loo,' I say loud enough so everyone can hear as I put my phone in my pocket.

I walk past the grown-ups talking. I try and look away, to make sure they don't catch on to what I'm about to do, but also avoid their stares so they don't think anything of me going, so that they don't start a mental timer on my bathroom visit.

I close the living-room door gently, but fully, behind me and look down the hallway.

I've done it. I'm . . . I'm doing it. I'm putting me first. I'm really . . . I'm really going to sneak out? Shit. Who even am I?!

The nerves are overwhelming now. But there's excitement seeping in too. I decide crawling out of the bathroom window is probably too risky. Don't want to get stuck or break a bone and end up in A & E or something. I'll just have to very carefully open and close the front door and sneak out that way. Annoying that I don't know how noisy their door is. Would be good to know how much pressure to apply, but I guess there's no point thinking about that now.

I grab my shoes and quickly start shoving them on.

'Since when do you need shoes to go to the toilet?' a voice asks behind me.

I quickly turn, falling against the wall.

I press my arm against the wall and right myself. 'Hamza . . . What . . . what are you doing out here?'

'Where you off to?'

Shit shit shit. I'm caught. It's over.

'I was just . . . I was . . .'

'God, you're chancing it, ain't ya?' He laughs a little. 'Look, it's fine. I know you're going to that comedy thing. I've been waiting all night to see if you'd miss it. Guess you proved me wrong.'

'Wait, what?' I blurt.

'I thought you'd just, y'know, give up. Like you always do.'

'Oh, ouch,' I reply sarcastically.

He rolls his eyes. 'You know it's true. This must be . . . This must be big if you're going to . . . sneak out for it.' He ends on a laugh.

'Right, well, no need to make fun,' I say, pushing up my glasses, trying not to show how hurt I am.

'No, that's not . . . I wasn't making fun.' He sighs, then looks around. He runs a hand through his hair, just like I always do. 'Look. It's fine. Like, go. Just go. I'll cover for you.'

'Wait, what? Really?'

What is happening? Who is this? This can't be the same brother who used to grass me up every time I ate one of the nice biscuits Ma kept for guests. 'Why . . . why would you do that?'

He shrugs a little, looks to the ground. 'You . . . you came to my match the other day. No one's ever come for me before. And that . . . Well, it was nice, that's all. To have someone there cheering for me.'

He's talking about the time I went to the match just to get his house keys. Just to get something that would help *me*. And now I feel like complete shit because I didn't even realise how much that might have meant to him, to have someone there at his games. The same way I want my family to support my stand-up efforts, maybe Hamza feels the same about his football matches.

'Like, I know you only came for the keys,' he continues, making me feel even worse. 'But it was just . . . yeah. I mean, you're the one who always makes sure my kit is clean and so . . . yeah, I guess I owe you. And it's . . . it's not like you're going off to do anything bad, or interesting. Nothing I can get you in big trouble for anyway. So it's fine, go. I'll cover.'

I stare at him for a few seconds, sure that this is a prank of some sort. That he's going to start laughing any second now. It's also the most open either of us has ever been with the other. It's not just my parents who don't do the emotional stuff in our family. Hamza and I might have been close as kids, but we've grown apart. This is without doubt . . . the nicest thing he's done for me in a while.

'You gonna go or what?' he says, running a hand through his hair again. 'Doesn't it start soon?'

He's . . . he's looked it up. There's no way he'd know about start

179

times, or even that it was on today, without doing his own research. There's no way he remembers that information from that quick glance at the poster he had the other day. I'm still confused as to why he suddenly cares so much, why he's suddenly being so nice.

'Oh my God, go!' he says, with a laugh that shows me he's not gonna take it back. 'Go through the back door – it'll be less obvious.'

I start nodding for some reason, relief flooding my body.

'Th-thanks,' I say, the word feeling weird in my mouth when addressed to Hamza.

He tips his chin up at me and I turn and walk towards the kitchen, where the back door is. I can't be sure, but it sounds like he mumbles, 'Good luck,' as he walks back into the living room.

The back door sounds loud as fuck. It creaks so loud I'm sure they can hear it from the living room. I have to do the thing where you open it inch by inch by inch. And then do the whole thing again in reverse to close it. Everything feels super loud, most of all my pounding heart. It's way more excitement than nerves now. Now that I'm outside, now that I don't have to worry about things with my parents. Now that I'm free.

The back door closes. I take a deep breath. It's dark out now, but not cold. Although that could be because I'm so hot from all the sneaking around. But the fresh air feels so good. It refreshes me. I just need to navigate my way through the back garden, around the side, through the gate and into the front garden, then sneak away without being seen through the window. Not hard at all. For real, the hard part is over.

I'm free.

I'm on my way to my dreams.

30

I text Dexter to tell him I'm on my way. I have enough time, even with Hamza's intervention and the back-garden stumbling. I don't need to run, like I thought I might. I imagine me bursting into the hall, through the doors, like people do in films when they're stopping a wedding. Except of course I'd never have the courage to do that. I'd probably just slip in through the back, all puffy from running the whole way, and quietly ask someone if I was a finalist.

But I'd do that at least.

I would. For stand-up. For my dream.

I'd do anything.

I start to feel lighter and lighter the further I get from Auntie Radiya's house. I don't know how I would have coped if Hamza hadn't offered to cover. I don't think I would have been able to relax all night.

I cross the road, following the map on my phone that's showing me a shortcut to the community centre. I don't like having my phone out in the dark, as it makes you more of a target for muggers, but I think I need those extra three minutes to take in the atmosphere of the event.

'Wait!' a voice calls out behind me.

My heart spikes in my chest. Did Ma find out? Did Hamza grass me up? Was that nice stuff all fake so he could go in and tell my parents so they would come after me? I turn around but can't see Ma chasing me with a rolling pin or anything.

Maybe I'm just so on edge, expecting it to happen, that I'm imagining it?

I look down at my map again and follow the arrows up a side street.

'COME BACK!!!' the voice calls again.

OK, I'm definitely not imagining it. And the voice sounds familiar. I backtrack my steps and look down the long road I just came up. I squint and see a small figure walk under one of the street lamps. Mariyam? No, it can't be. I push my glasses up my nose and look closer, waiting for them to pass another street light.

Just then my phone buzzes. It's so unexpected, and I'm so tense that I almost drop it. It's a text from Hamza.

Think Mariyam saw u leaving n run out after u! Find her!!!!!

Shit shit shit.

'Mariyam!?' I scream into the darkness.

'Bhaiyya!' her voice calls back. She's close.

'Mariyam, what are you doing?!' I ask.

'WHAT?!' she shouts, unable to hear me because of a nearby car with a loud exhaust.

I finally see her right across the road from me, and relief floods my body. Thank God she's OK. Anything could have happened. I knew I shouldn't have chanced this. Nothing good was ever going to come of it, was it? This is the universe again, saying, *Screw you. You're not meant to be a comedian. You're not meant to win this competition. You're not meant to follow your dreams.*

I quickly start texting back Hamza as I make my way up to the kerb. I'm two words into the message when I hear Mariyam squeal my name again. I look up and watch as she steps off the onto the street, not looking before she crosses.

'Bhaiyya, I missed you!' she yells, just before a car horn blares.

There's a screech of brakes and then a loud thud as a car slams right into my little sister.

31

The lights in the hospital waiting room are so bright it hurts. It's so noisy in here too – people screaming, crying, someone in the corner puking. But I deserve this.

Mariyam had to be rushed to A & E in an ambulance because of me. She's through those locked double doors right now, being treated by God knows how many doctors. I barely remember anything, it happened so fast. Just Hamza running out, screaming. Me screaming. The woman in the car getting out and screaming. But silence from Mariyam. The person who should have been making the most noise was completely silent. Completely still. Everyone suddenly appeared, running, and I don't even know who called the ambulance. But before I knew it, Ma was having to be held back by the paramedics so they could load Mariyam into the ambulance, Baba too was shouting in broken English for them to help his daughter, and I was just standing there, doing nothing. There was nothing I *could* do. I'd done enough.

This is all my fault.

If she dies. If anything happens to her, it will be all my

fault. My selfishness is the reason she's hurt. I'm so fucking stupid. I should have just let it go. Should have just taken the trip to Auntie Radiya's house as a sign that I should stop with this stupid dream, this stupid idea that I can make anything of myself doing stand-up. I should have just stayed with my family. Stayed on that sofa playing games with Mariyam. There's no point trying to find facts to support the idea that it might not be my fault. There's no denying it. This is all because of me.

'Why are they taking so long?' Hamza shouts, suddenly stopping his pacing and kicking an empty chair.

'Hamza!' Uncle Mustafa and Auntie Radiya chime at the same time.

Hamza glares at them both. I've never seen him so agitated. 'They should have told us something by now,' he says, his voice still at a loud enough level that everyone around us can hear.

'I'm sure she'll be fine,' Uncle Mustafa says. 'She was awake when they took her in. That's a good thing. Your parents are with her too. She'll be OK.'

'We just need to sit here and pray,' Auntie Radiya says. She holds her palms out in the prayer position and looks up at me. 'Ibrahim, come, sit and pray with us.'

Hamza whips his head to look at me, frowns. He blames me too. As he should. Everyone should. I shouldn't even be here. I'm probably making things worse just by my presence. Like a karmic balance thing. Pure, sweet little Mariyam can't get any better until I leave. Until I stop being such a selfish prick.

It's my fault.

All my fault.

The tears start to flow again. Everything had dried up after the initial shock. On the drive over, watching those flashing blue lights in front of us, feeling like the life might be draining out of her with every flash of the light, every cycle of the siren.

I can't get it out of my head.

'I'm going to sneak in,' I say, standing up. I need to see her. I need to make sure she's OK. I need to make sure . . .

'Yeah, you're really good at sneaking places, aren't you?' Hamza says snidely.

No one knows the truth about why I was out. Hamza never told them, never grassed me up, and in the panic no one has asked. Maybe they thought I chased Mariyam out, or that she was with me in the first place. If they knew the truth, they'd hate me as much as Hamza does.

'They're not going to let you in,' Auntie Radiya says. 'They said two people per patient, remember? Your parents will tell us when there's anything to say. The doctors know what they're doing, Ibrahim. *Sabr*, remember? Be patient. Come on, come sit down and pray with me.'

'No,' I say more forcefully than I meant to. 'No no no. I need to . . . I need to go see her. I need to make this better.'

'Oh, just shut up,' Hamza says, all traces of his niceness from earlier gone. 'You can't make anything better. You just make things worse. Just leave. We're better off without you. This wouldn't have happened if you hadn't . . .' He trails off, his voice on the verge of tears.

He's right. He's so fucking right. They are better off without me. I can feel the panic rising up inside me, but no . . . I don't have time for that now. It can't happen now. I try to take deep

186

breaths, the way Sura showed me. I try to imagine her standing in front of me, breathing with me. But it doesn't work. All I can see is Mariyam bouncing off that car bonnet. All I can hear is that sickening thud, the screams afterwards.

I can't. Can't can't can't deal with this.

My breaths start getting shallower, harder.

This is all my fault. I made everything terrible. I can't do anything right.

You just make things worse.
Just leave.
We're better off without you.

I can feel everyone staring at me, can feel the dread, the anxiety, the panic, all rising up within me like a tidal wave. It's going to pour out any second now.

My vision has black spots now, and my legs are jelly.

It's happening and there's nothing I can do to stop it.

You just make things worse.
Just leave.
We're better off without you.

Hamza's words are seared on my mind, echoing all around.

I'm going to die.

And I deserve it.

I did this to Mariyam, so this is what I deserve.

My family would be so much better off without me. None of this would be happening if I'd never been born. Things would be so much better.

The panic is rising, so high that I know I need to get out. I don't want to leave Mariyam but . . .

I'm about to die.

For real.

Anyway, I only make things worse for the people I love.

I turn to the doors and run.

32

I look up and realise that during my panic attack I've somehow left the hospital grounds and ended up . . . on a bridge over the motorway.

How the fuck did I get here? What . . . Why the hell did I come here? I whip my head back and forth, as if there'll be an explanation nearby. But there's just darkness. A lorry passes below me, making the bridge tremble. I look over the railing and watch the rear lights fade into the darkness. I realise it's started raining.

A memory of the last time I was in this exact spot comes to my mind. It was the day that Dexter's mum died. While the doctors were operating on her, trying to save her, Dexter said he needed a walk, and we somehow ended up here. I was trying super hard to distract him, and I remember we made up a game where we would look at the people in the cars stuck in traffic and make up funny stories about their lives. The woman singing loudly in her car was secretly a drug dealer who had a stash in her boot. The old man with the bushy beard was a

Santa impersonator who worked at a phone-sex company in the off-season.

I remember thinking I was doing a good job distracting Dexter from everything. But soon I was the only one playing. I looked over to Dexter and saw him leaning really far over the railing, looking down. At the time I thought he was just trying to hide his tears.

Soon after, Dexter's dad called, telling us to come back.

I put my feet on the bottom of the railing and lean over. I see it now. What Dexter saw. What went through his head back then.

Wondering whether it would hurt, to go this way. Wondering how quickly life leaves a body. How quickly we turn from a person into nothingness. Wondering what it will be like on the other side. Knowing that this would be such a huge relief. A way out from all the pain.

I throw a leg over the railing so I'm straddling it, then pull my other leg across. I rearrange myself so I'm standing facing the oncoming traffic. The only thing keeping me from plummeting to the ground is my sweaty grip on the bar behind me.

Maybe this is what the panic attacks have been trying to tell me all along. Maybe this is the reason my subconscious brought me here.

This is the answer.

33

'Ibrahim, no!'

I whip my head around, panicked. Sura stands there, in her trademark electric-blue scarf and black polka-dot dress.

'Sura?' I ask, surprised. 'What . . . what are you doing here? *How* are you here?'

All those times I needed her and she didn't turn up because she said I had to come to her? Making me break into the community centre at night when she could have come to me? What the fuck?

'Ibrahim, please,' she begs. 'Please come back over to this side. I need . . . I need to keep you safe, OK? You can't . . . You can't do this.'

There's something different about her today. Her voice . . . There's panic in her voice. I've never seen her anything but composed. She's always in good spirits, always perky. Annoyingly so. And yet today is totally different. Her eyes keep flitting from my face to the railing, down to the road.

'This is the best thing,' I say, following her gaze down to the wet tarmac. 'Everything is going to shit because of me, and isn't this the *only* answer? The only way to get things to be good? Mariyam's in hospital because of me. God knows what's going to happen to her.'

I expect her to tell me Mariyam's going to be OK. That she's in the best place to get help. But she's just looking at me, sadness all over her face. Sura knows everything, she's shown me things only a . . . a higher being would know. She would be able to tell me if Mariyam's going to be OK. She would know. So the fact she's not saying anything of the sort terrifies me.

'That wasn't your fault, Ibrahim,' she says instead, after a few seconds.

'Yes, it was!' I shout. 'She followed me out. It was all because I was being a selfish prick, putting my desire to do stand-up over my family.'

'Ibrahim, you're the *opposite* of selfish. You put everyone's needs above yours.'

'Right, and that's not helping me either, is it?' I ask. 'I just . . . I can't deal with it any more, Sura. The pressure of having everything on my shoulders, of always having to worry about my parents, my siblings, the finances, the house, their health. I can't stop worrying about all of it. I can't stop wondering when things are next going to go wrong, and how I can stop them. It's like . . . I just . . . I want to live for myself. I want to put myself first for once. And that's selfish as fuck, isn't it? They need my help. My parents . . . they don't cope like other kids' parents. And I . . . I resent them for that. I really do. And that makes me feel like such a prick because I know they've done so much for me, and they're my *parents*, y'know? I *should* be helping them out where I can. But it just . . . it feels like too much. I just . . . I want someone to look after me, rather than

192

me having to look after everyone else. And that's not . . . that's not possible. Not with the way my parents are, my family is. So it's just . . . it's better this way.'

'Ibrahim!' She half shouts my name as I shuffle a bit on the ledge. 'This bad period you're having? It will pass. You've survived every panic attack, every bad moment so far. You can survive this too. I *promise*, the way you're feeling now, it's not going to last forever.' Sura's speaking fast now, urgently.

'You can't know that!' I shout, gripping the railing tighter. There are tears running down my face now. I wish she hadn't come. It would have been done by now if she hadn't disturbed me. It would have been so much better already.

'It's so easy for you to spout this bullshit,' I spit. 'You haven't . . . you haven't been through this. You can't understand how it feels. How *I* feel. You don't have a clue.'

'I *do*,' she says. Fiercely, loudly, sternly. I turn back to her and she's got a troubled look on her face. Her brow is set, she looks . . . determined somehow. But also pained. As if she's reliving an awful memory.

'I know *exactly* what you're feeling,' she says. 'We're so alike, you and me . . . I know what it's like to feel so desperate . . . to be literally on the edge. Not for the same reasons as you, but I've also felt like this is the only answer.' Then she . . . lets out a little laugh. A bitter, one-note laugh, as she looks at the railing I'm still holding onto, looks past the railing to the motorway below. 'I've been *exactly* where you are, and then –' she looks back at me . . . pierces me with her watery stare – 'and then . . . a stranger, somebody who was good and kind . . . reminded me of the things I had to be thankful for, the things I had to *live* for. He showed me the truths I had been blind to because of my depression. Made me believe that things would get better.' She pauses and looks straight at me. 'And they did, Ibrahim. Trust me, the same will happen for you.'

'This isn't going to work,' I say quietly, more to myself than to her. 'You're not going to change my mind this time.' I look down at the road. I can see a lorry approaching, its headlights still just tiny dots in the distance.

This is it.

This is the one.

'We tried. *You* tried, a lot. To help me, and, uh, thank you for that,' I tell her. 'But my problems can't be fixed with rational thinking or meditation and being in the moment. It's . . . it's bigger than that. It's . . . harder than that. You can tell me as much as you want that I have a positive impact on people in my life, or whatever. But it's not . . . it's not enough. I need more. I just . . .' I sigh, watch the lorry come closer and closer. 'Don't you get it? *I'm* what's wrong. I'm not worth saving. Nothing is going to get better, because *I'm* the problem. I'm –'

'No,' she says sternly, resolutely. She takes a step towards me. The lorry's coming closer. I need to do this, but the tone in her voice stops me. I look at her.

'You're *not* the problem, Ibrahim. No one is unfixable. Everyone is worth saving. You're going to . . . you're going to do so many great things. There's so much ahead of you, I promise. And if you're not going to take my word for it then . . . then let me show you!'

194

34

The lorry passes below us, the tyres hissing in the rain. I'm staring at Sura now instead.

'What . . . what do you mean?' I ask tentatively.

As soon as I say it, I know she's going to say 'Magic, remember?' and I wait for it, anger bubbling up, waiting for her to say it so I can let my fury out on her. So that I can get this whole conversation, this pathetic attempt to stop me, over and done with and just find the next lorry.

But she doesn't say that. Even though she's said that every other time. She's so . . . serious today. More so than I've ever seen her. Not just serious, panicked almost. Sura always seems to have a grasp on things, be so sure of everything, but it seems like her finding me here, about to do this has . . . rattled her.

There are no smiles, no little jokes, no pep in her voice. It just reinforces the fact that everything is terrible because of me. Before, she was fine, happy. And now I've infected her too.

'I can't show you a *definitive* future,' she says, stepping a smidge closer, 'as that will change based on every tiny decision you make. But . . . I can show you what your life . . . *could* be . . . if you decide to hold on. If you just agree to wait for this to pass, I can show you what your future could look like.' Her voice is soft now, and I'm drawn in, intrigued, though my fingers are still clenched around the metal railing.

'Close your eyes and picture the scenarios I'll describe to you,' Sura says. This will help, trust me.'

I just stare at her, my face stinging from the wind against the trail of my tears, torn between doing what she says and just throwing myself off this bridge right now. Just the fall from this distance should be enough, right? Who even needs a lorry?

'Just . . . trust me,' Sura repeats, as if she can sense what I'm thinking. 'I need you to trust me just one more time.'

I reluctantly nod, then turn to look out over the road. I'll do what she says, but it doesn't mean I have to look at her.

'Think about all the things you could do with your life,' Sura says softly. 'There are literally countless possibilities. Just . . . imagine being centre stage at the Apollo, like you've always dreamed of . . .'

As soon as she says it, the image pops into my head, so vivid and real it's as if I'm living it, not just seeing it in my head. There's me in a checked blue shirt, standing in the spotlight, an audience of thousands facing me. The idea of it sends a shiver through me. There's a smile on my face as I pace around the stage, talking easily. Not just a smile, a grin. I look . . . happy. No nerves, no anxiety, nothing. Just pure elation. I say something, a joke, part of my routine, and the audience bursts into laughter. My face lights up at the reaction, and the warmth of it spreads to the real me, the me imagining this future. It's as if I'm watching a memory rather than a premonition.

'Or maybe you'd have your own TV show,' Sura says, still in that soft, dreamlike voice.

As soon as she says it, the vision in my head changes. Still super bright and vivid and still like I'm actually living it, rather than imagining it. This time I'm on a TV set, wearing the same outfit as in the last vision, the same shirt I'm wearing right now, I realise. I'm standing in front of a couple of cameras, and other members of crew. I can see myself more clearly in this vision for some reason. I realise I'm older here. Not like *old* old. Maybe in my thirties. A woman comes over and brushes some make-up powder on my forehead and nose. She's so close I feel the urge to step back, but the me in this vision doesn't do that. Instead he smiles at her, says something that makes her burst out laughing. He smiles. He's not fidgeting, he's . . . making eye contact with her and everything. This doesn't feel like it could ever be me, and yet, at the same time . . . it feels like it *could* be. We start filming and it turns out to be the kind of show where someone – me – talks about clips in the news and provides some witty commentary. There's no audience here, but the crew burst out laughing at some of my jokes.

'There'll be things to look forward to outside of comedy too,' Sura says. 'Outside of your work. Your personal life will be fulfilling too. Maybe you'll find a partner, have children . . .'

My head fills with an image of a big green field, dotted with the tiny white flowers Mariyam always makes necklaces out of. I'm in the distance this time, but I know it's me. An even older version of me. I'm standing up, a football by my foot. Next to me is a picnic blanket, where a woman sits, surrounded by snacks and sandwiches. Her back is turned to me so I can't see her face, but I can tell she's got a baby in her arms. A happy shriek lights up the memory, and a little girl comes running up to me, decked out in an Arsenal kit. She tries to sneak the ball from me, but I kick it away, eliciting another happy shriek from her. The sound makes present me, real me, smile. An ache runs through me. A desire to have this. To feel this happiness. To have someone who loves me. I can feel the tears prick at the corner of my eyes even though they're closed.

'And your family, Ibrahim,' Sura continues, softer than ever. 'They need you to stick around. Not just for the services you provide, or the ways in which you help them out. Not just because of what you can do *for* them. They love you, Ibrahim. They need you there. They . . . love having you around. You're the only one who can make them laugh, cheer them up when they're down . . .'

Another image comes into my mind, another vivid premonition. Ma, Baba, Mariyam, Hamza and me sitting at the dining table, all of us a bit older than we are now. We're playing Monopoly. There's a stack of money in the middle of the board, ready for someone to land on Free Parking and take it all. Mariyam's blowing on the dice, doing her little prayer, like she always does. She's about ten in this vision. It's weird to see her so grown-up, so much taller. Weird to see her moving her piece across the board without having to count every square. Everyone looks so . . . happy. Mariyam lands on a property that belongs to Ma. This is usually when Ma asks one of us to read her property card to figure out how much rent is due, but now . . . now she just glances at her card and reads it off easily. She smirks at Mariyam, holding her hand out for payment. The whole scene is just so lovely . . . so loving. So happy.

'This could all be real, Ibrahim,' Sura says. 'Everything I've shown you, it's all possible. They're all versions of your possible future. It's . . . it's within your reach. It won't all be sunshine and happiness, of course. That's life. We all have our ups and downs – it's what makes us human. But . . . but there is so much good coming your way. I *promise*, Ibrahim. I promise it's worth you holding on. Just a little bit longer.'

35

'Ibrahim?'

My eyes are still closed, my fingers still wrapped around the railing behind me, still listening to Sura's words, but Sura's voice has changed. It doesn't sound like her any more. Doesn't even sound like a girl's voice. I swivel my head towards the voice, opening my eyes to find . . .

'Dexter?' I ask, feeling as if my heart has literally stopped.

His eyes are wide and panicked, his gaze flitting between my face and my fingers tight around the metal bar.

'Ib . . . ! What . . . ? Get . . . get down from there.' His voice is shaking, the whites of his eyes large and bright in the darkness.

I twist around and hoist myself back over, my entire body sagging with relief as my feet hit the sturdy ground.

'Dex . . . what are . . . what are you doing here?' I look around, trying to find where Sura went, but of course she's disappeared just as quickly as she came. Like she always does. But Dexter's standing in the exact same position as her. It's as if she transformed into him.

'I was worried about you, mate. When you didn't turn up, I tried calling you. I know you said you were having some family stuff, but I called and I called and I called and you didn't answer. I got . . . I got worried so I tracked your phone location. When it showed me you were here, I freaked out and rushed over.'

'But . . . but you'll miss your shot at winning. You were . . . you would've won, Dex. Why would you throw that away?'

The feelings of panic start up again, realising that once again I've ruined someone's life. Dexter was worried about me, because I'm an idiot who doesn't answer his phone. He abandoned his chance to follow his dreams . . . all because I'm a pathetic mess.

'Who cares about winning?' he says. 'You would have done the same if you were worried about me, if I'd gone missing. The plan was always me and you till the end, remember? Together, or not at all. From my side anyway – dunno if you would have screwed me over.'

He stops, flashes me an attempt at a jokey grin, before looking back down at the road as a lorry speeds by. I panic, trying to think of what to say, how to explain this all.

'What are you doing here?' he asks quietly. 'Why were you on the . . . on the other side of the railing? Mate, are you . . . are you OK?'

Now it's my turn to put on the fake smile. The mask I put on when I'm onstage. At least I try to, but it's just . . . so much effort tonight. As if it's taking everything inside me to get my face to cooperate. I look his way, but slightly over his shoulder. I would crumple if I looked into his eyes.

I hold the painful smile and reply, 'I'm fine.'

'You're obviously not fine,' he says. He steps forward, puts his hand on my upper arm. His touch feels so weird, as if it shocks me, fires up my body. But not in a good way. I feel my defences crumbling. I feel every single thing inside me turning to liquid, everything just breaking down, and then, before I even know what's happening, I'm crying again. Not just normal crying, but ugly, gross, pathetic, embarrassing crying. I let out some sort of cross between an animal noise and a snotty snort, and then just completely break down. I literally collapse onto the ground, kneeling on the pavement, wanting to just curl up into a ball.

I can't . . . I can't do this any more.

Dexter must think I'm fucking crazy. But it's too hard. Keeping it all in, trying to deal with all this on my own, in my stupid head. It's all too much.

'Whoa, fuck, Ibrahim, what's the matter, mate?' There's more panic in his voice now, and he's lowered himself to the ground too, kneeling in front of me. 'Talk to me,' he says. 'What's going on? Do I need to get you some help?'

He sounds so . . . caring. His voice is laced with worry, and while that makes me anxious because I made him like that, it also touches my heart a bit. We don't do this kind of touchy-feely stuff, so when Dexter pulls me into a hug and says, 'It's gonna be OK, mate. Whatever it is. It's going to be OK.' I break down even more, wrapping my arms around him, burying my face into his shoulder, snotting all over the nice shirt he picked out for the final before the competition even started. His words . . . his tone . . . everything is just so comforting. I thought he'd feel awkward about seeing me like this. That he'd back away so fast. But he isn't . . . he's doing the opposite. He's being . . . he's being exactly what I need right now.

There's a tiny part of me that's embarrassed at how pathetic I'm being. But it's tiny. My body is just overwhelmed with warmth from Dexter's hug. I hang on to him tighter and let it out, let out all my tears, all my snot. And to his credit, he doesn't get scared off, he doesn't joke about what a pussy I'm being, or how I'm ruining his clothes. He just . . . sits there, holding me, letting me cry. And that means the world right now.

I don't know how long we sit on that bridge, arms around each other, me just sobbing. The tears do stop eventually though, as does the rain. I raise my head and he pulls back. I wipe my nose with the back of my hand, waiting for the awkwardness to seep in. I don't think Dexter and I have ever hugged, not even when his mum died. I feel like I should thank him for coming, for showing up when I needed him, for sitting with me, letting me slobber all over him in sadness. But . . . I can't find the words.

'Talk to me, mate,' he says as we both sit down properly on the damp ground, backs against the railings, the rumble of cars going beneath us every few seconds. 'What's . . . what's going on? What's happened?'

I turn to look at him, expecting him to be smirking at me, or making a joke of it, but his face doesn't show any of that. He looks . . . concerned. Genuinely concerned.

I might not be able to talk to my family about what I'm feeling, the pressure, the sadness, the panic and anxiety, but Dexter . . . I could talk to him, right? He's just seen me at my worst, seen me going through it. He hasn't made a single joke yet, and I embarrassed the fuck out of myself . . .

203

And I need someone. I realise that now. Sura's too flaky. I need someone real. Someone who's always around, who is there for me. And the only person in my life who's always been there for me when I needed them . . . is Dexter.

'I've . . . I've been . . . really . . . struggling . . . a lot . . .' I say slowly, carefully, quietly.

There's still that expectation that he'll burst out laughing, but he doesn't.

'Tell me about it,' he says instead. 'I'm listening.'

36

We talk for a while, and every word that comes out of my mouth makes me feel so much lighter. I know Dexter can't fully understand everything – the way I don't think anyone outside of my culture and religion would be able to fully understand the unspoken rules we have, the way we're expected above everything to value, respect and serve our parents. That we always have to put family above everything. But I tell Dexter about it anyway. I tell him about my parents needing me to do the simplest things for them, and how I can't help but compare them to everyone else's parents, who act like actual adults and do all the things adults do, like take care of the bills and medical stuff. I tell him about the pressure I feel to keep things afloat, that I feel like I have to always put their needs above mine, and how it's exhausting me. Then I tell him about how *those* feelings make me feel like the most selfish prick in the world, and then that makes things even worse. I tell him about my panic attacks, what they feel like, and how they've now started coming on with no trigger. I don't tell him about Sura, of course. That might make him think I'm clinically insane, and maybe he'd try and get me sectioned.

Although . . . the way he's listening, the way he's nodding along, chiming in with the appropriate things, I don't think he'd do something like that. It seems like . . . like he sees what's happening, like he can understand, if not completely, enough to get the gist of why I feel like this. Sitting next to him, talking this all out . . . God, it feels cathartic. As if this is exactly what I needed, to just get it all out, have my best friend listen and comfort me.

'Shit, man,' Dexter says when I run out of things to say. His voice isn't awkward and embarrassed, like I thought it would be. Like I worried it would be. He just sounds like . . . like Dexter when he's being real. His voice sounds the way it did in the scene Sura showed me where he opened up to his dad about how much he was grieving.

'That's so much on you. So rough. I can't believe you've been dealing with so much. That you felt so bad that you thought you should . . .' He trails off, but looks out towards the motorway, where the cars keep driving on by, oblivious to what's happening up here.

'Yeah . . .' I say. I run a hand through my hair and tug. 'It's just . . . it's been a lot. And then today, with Mariyam, her getting hurt . . . I couldn't . . . I can't deal with it all any more. It's too much.'

'She's going to be fine, Ib,' Dexter reassures. 'You said she was awake when they took her in, right? That's a good sign. I'm sure she's going to be OK.'

As if on cue, my phone starts ringing.

'It's Dad,' I say, a spike of fear striking up in my heart, in my head. I jump up off the ground. 'Something bad must have happened.'

I stare at the screen, bright and loud with the word 'DAD'. I know I should answer it, that he probably has some news about Mariyam, but . . . I'm terrified. And if I don't answer it, I won't have to know the badness. The badness won't be happening.

'Why do you always assume it's bad?' Dexter asks, standing up and brushing the dirt off his jeans. 'You won't know what it is until you answer, and surely it's better to know?'

'No way,' I say. 'So much better to live in ignorance.' I say it a bit jokingly, but I totally do believe it. Thankfully the phone stops ringing then. There's so many missed calls and texts on my screen. I can't bear to look at them.

'You can't keep running away from bad things,' Dexter says, not joining in my small attempts to go back to our jokey norm. His voice is still all serious. 'The only way to properly get through things is to . . . live them. To have the hard conversations. It makes things better, I promise. I actually . . . I actually had something similar with my dad recently. You remember that day you were at mine? With the photos and the jokes about her being in a coffin?'

'Oh God, yeah, Dexter I'm so sorry about that,' I say quickly, cringing at the memory.

'No, no, don't apologise. It was actually really helpful . . . It triggered this whole conversation with Dad. We spoke about Mum, and we realised that we hadn't really properly grieved for her, neither of us, which is why he was hiding her away all the time. Anyway, I'm just saying, it was . . . it was *hard* talking about it, but things are *so* much better now.'

The smallest things can indeed make a huge difference.

I don't think I had bought any of what Sura said about my part in all this until just now. Until it came right from Dexter's mouth.

'Trust me on this, mate,' Dexter says, putting a hand on my shoulder. 'Keeping things bottled up never helps anyone. You need to let it out. Talk to someone – maybe a therapist?' He must notice me pulling a face because he quickly continues. 'But if you don't want that, I'm here for you. For real. Always. I know it's not . . . Like, I know we're not the mushy touchy-feely type, but mate . . . I'm worried about you. You shouldn't struggle like this on your own. I'm *always* here for you. And I promise . . . I can be serious, right? Look!' He pulls a strained face, eyes comically wide open, mouth in a straight line.

I burst out laughing. God, Dexter is amazing at making me feel better. Maybe he is the answer. I don't know why I didn't try this before. It's nowhere near as awkward as I thought it would be to talk about this stuff to him. I guess with Sura it was easy because she was a stranger, and not real. I wouldn't have to live with it if it ever got too dark and heavy and weird. But turns out that there are people in this world, in my life, who won't run after seeing my full truth.

'Thanks, mate,' I reply when the laughter fades away and we're both just smiling. 'That really means a lot.' I want to say more. Want to tell him how *much* it means to me, how I'm so relieved to have him in my life. How grateful I am for him. But I think that would be veering into *too* mushy for right now. So instead I just lightly shove him on the shoulder and say, 'You're the best.'

My phone goes off again, but with a text this time. From Hamza.

Where r u? Everyone's gon crazy looking 4 u. Mariyam's fine – just a broken arm. Come back. She's asking for you.

37

Dexter and I continue to chat as we walk to the hospital. I tell him how I felt too embarrassed to talk to him about any of this stuff earlier, and he says he felt the same. He thought he shouldn't talk about his grief because it would make him look soft, then tells me more about how he misses his mum. It feels good to have him talk to me about his emotions. Makes me feel less guilty about offloading all my crap on him. It also feels like our friendship is stronger because of it.

As we walk up the path to A & E though, my heart starts pounding. I don't know what's going to happen in there. I just know it's going to be bad. It's good news that Mariyam is OK, but my parents are still going to be so mad, especially since Hamza has probably told them that she was following me.

'I'll wait for you here,' Dexter says as we walk into the waiting room. 'It's gonna be OK, mate. Right? You're . . . you're tough, Mariyam's tough, you can both get through this.'

I smile at him, blushing a little at his compliment. 'Thanks, man,' I reply quietly.

And then, before I know it, he's wrapping me into another hug. The waiting room is half full, and it feels a bit awkward with people around us, but I hug him back. Tight. He goes to sit in front of the TV on the wall, where the news is playing. It's the same spot Auntie Radiya and Uncle Mustafa were sitting. No sign of them now. They probably went home after hearing Mariyam was OK.

I spot Hamza by the vending machine. He leans down, picks up his drink from the bottom flap, then straightens up. As he turns around, our eyes meet. He's not that far away from me, and I can see his eyes are a bit red. Hamza isn't the type to cry over anything. If Mariyam's OK, why . . . why are his eyes like that?

'Is . . . is everything OK?' I ask. I look into his face and then back towards the locked doors that go towards the patient beds. 'Mariyam –'

'She's fine,' Hamza says quickly, noticing the panic on my face. There's a softness to his voice that I haven't heard before. There's also a sense of relief in there, the lightness he only has after we've had a fight and he comes to ask if I want something to eat, as a way of making up.

'What *happened* to you?' He's looking at me hard, as if there's something on my face, so I instinctively push my glasses up my nose and then wipe my cheeks again, just in case there's still some tears there. 'Where did you go?' he asks. There's a tinge of anger there, and it rises as he continues. 'After *everything*, did you run off to that stupid competition?'

'No! God, no!' I reply, anger flaring in me too, that he would think I would do that with Mariyam in the hospital.

'Where did you go then?' Hamza asks again, less angry this time. 'We've been calling you for ages.'

211

'I just . . . I needed some air,' I reply quietly, looking down at the floor. I run a hand through my hair and tug. 'It was . . . it was getting a bit much. I felt so . . . guilty. It's all my fault, what happened to her. You were right.'

'No, dude, I was . . .' His voice is quiet, and he can't meet my eye. He looks down to the ground and tugs on his ear. 'I was out of order saying all that. I was just . . . scared about Mariyam.'

Hamza's never *ever* admitted he was wrong. This is weird. This isn't like us. But that doesn't mean it's a bad thing. Dexter said talking things out is always good, and so Hamza showing a new side, showing some emotions . . . that's good, right? A little awkward but . . . good. It makes me think things might actually be able to change.

'Is she . . . ? Is she OK?' I ask, looking back to the locked doors, wondering what's going on behind there. 'Like, *really* OK?'

'Yeah, yeah, she's fine,' Hamza replies. 'She's got a broken arm though, so she'll probably be bossing us around even more than usual and making us do everything for her for a few weeks.'

Relief floods through me. We both chuckle, share a look, then awkwardly look away.

'She's been asking for you non-stop,' Hamza says more quietly.

My heart constricts a little, and I'm suddenly desperate to see her. As if Hamza can sense this, he jerks his head towards the door and says, 'C'mon.'

Hamza opens the blue curtains to Mariyam's bay, and I catch a glimpse of her lying on the bed, her plastered arm across her chest. But before I can take her in properly, or say anything to her, Ma's up out of her chair and is rushing over to me.

'Oh thank God!' she says. 'I was so worried something had happened to you too,' she says, wrapping her arms around me. Tight. It's . . . weirding me out. To see her so emotional, about me. To hear that she was worried. About *me*. What is happening with my family today? Since when did they become so sentimental and weirdly caring? I guess this is what a scare like tonight does to a family.

'I'm sorry,' I say to Ma as I hug her back. 'I'm sorry I didn't answer the phone. Sorry I ran off.'

She pulls away from me and I see that her eyes are red and tired, like Hamza's. 'I'm just glad you're OK.'

I can't help but wonder how she would react if she knew where I was, what I was about to do. Although I don't think I could *ever* deal with her knowing, deal with having to explain what led me to that place. Tonight has made me realise that I do need help. Maybe even the professional kind (still not into the idea of a therapist). I can't keep dealing with all the panic and anxiety on my own. I think I need to start that process of understanding it all myself, of starting that journey, before talking to my family about it. If I ever decide to. In the meantime, at least I know I can talk to Dexter. Just knowing he's there and he will listen calms my brain so much. Brings me so much peace.

I turn to Mariyam. She looks so small in that huge bed, drowned by the blankets. But there's still a slight smile on her face.

'Hey, you,' I say as I walk over. I bend over and kiss her on the forehead. 'How are you doing?'

'It hurts,' she says feebly. I can hear tears coming.

'But your cast is so cool!' I say, forced pep in my voice. 'Did they let you pick the colour?'

'Yeah!' she says. 'Hamza tried to get me to pick blue, but I said, "No way, Jose!" Yellow is the best.'

'You're right, it's perfect,' I say, idly stroking her cast. It feels weirdly damp and cold.

'Hamza said I can get everyone at school to sign it, and that they'll all bring me sweets so I feel better.' She's definitely perked up now. What a kid. I look over to Hamza, and he's just looking at her, smiling. Weird to see him so emotional, weird to see him smiling at all.

'Where did you go?' Baba asks. His voice is different too. I can't tell if I detect a hint of anger in his words.

'Sorry,' I say again. I run a hand through my hair, tug on it. 'I just . . . I felt so bad. Mariyam got hurt because of me. I couldn't . . . I couldn't handle it, so I went for a walk. I needed some space. I'm sorry, I should have said. I should have answered your calls, but I just . . .' I trail off.

'Where did you even go in the first place?' Ma asks, a new sense of suspicion in her voice. 'Why did you leave Radiya's?'

My heart lurches. I had thought she would just forget that, move on and just want to focus on Mariyam getting better, but I guess not.

Before I can decide whether to tell the truth or lie, Hamza chirps up.

'He said he was going out to get some fresh air,' Hamza

says quickly. 'He wasn't feeling well, were you?' He looks at me, gives me a pointed stare. I'm supposed to agree with him. Supposed to follow his lie, because it would definitely get me out of this conversation.

But I realise I can't do that.

If I want things to change, then I need to change things. I'm done with hiding my passions. Hiding my true self. Be the change you wanna see and all that.

'No, that's not . . .' I turn away from Hamza's look of confusion to my parents who are also slightly baffled. I take a deep breath. 'I . . . I had an event I wanted to go to. I *had* to . . . It was the finals of that . . . comedy competition I'm part of. It was a big deal for me. I couldn't miss it.'

'You snuck out of your aunt's house to go to a . . . comedy competition?' Ma asks.

'I . . . I tried telling you I couldn't go to Auntie Radiya's, but . . . you wouldn't listen. It was . . . it was the finals today. I wanted to . . . I just . . . It's something I'm really passionate about. It was important to me, and you wouldn't understand, so I thought the only thing to do was to . . . sneak out. I'm sorry. I didn't realise . . . I didn't think Mariyam would follow me, or that anything like this would happen.'

'No way you could've known,' Hamza says. I shoot him a small grateful smile. 'This little brat is unpredictable,' he says. He lightly pushes Mariyam's head, and she grins.

'The only thing that matters is that Mariyam is OK,' Baba says, turning from me back to the bed. 'We can talk about everything else later.'

Later.

215

Later is something, I guess. Maybe Baba will support me. Maybe he could end up being like Dexter's dad.

Or maybe he'll tell me off for even entertaining the idea of following such a useless career path. Tell me that I need to be a man and find a job that can support our family.

But later is also a promise. Of a conversation, at the very least. And I know now what happens when I keep putting everyone else above my own needs. I know now that things need to change.

38

Mariyam is the worst patient in the world. She's over the moon with her bright yellow cast, especially after it gets filled up with doodles and signatures from her classmates, but at home it's like she's on her deathbed. She spends every afternoon the first week spread across the sofa, asking me, Ma, or Hamza even more than usual for something to 'help her heal'. No matter that these things include bad snacks, dolls and felt-tip pens. It's annoying for sure, but I'm just thankful she's OK, that she's feeling well enough to be her mischievous self. Even if that does mean me bringing her biscuits five times a day.

I think I'm doing a bit better too. That night on the bridge really did scare some sense into me. I don't . . . I don't want to ever go back to feeling like that, and now I know that, if I just let things carry on like before, it probably will happen again. So I'm forcing myself to make some changes. And the first step to that is actually asking for proper help.

'And then you just press send down the bottom there,' Dexter says, pointing to the bottom of my laptop screen. 'Then they'll get a therapist to read your referral, call you, talk it over and see how they can help you.'

'Huh, how weird,' I say, clicking the button before I can change my mind. 'I always thought you had to go to the doctor for stuff like this.'

The screen flashes with a confirmation message. I've done it. I've actually referred myself to the well-being service for some help with my mental health.

'I think it might still be worth doing that?' Dexter says, switching from lying on his stomach to sitting cross-legged on my bed. 'They might give you some medication or something. Shall we book you an appointment? Or do you wanna see how this well-being thing goes first?'

'Yeah, one step at a time,' I say, shutting the laptop so I don't have to look at it any more, so that I can't second-guess what's going to happen. I've done the right thing. I know I have. Things need to change. The things that have changed already have been for the best. I mean, talking to Dexter about stuff has been . . . really amazing. He's like a Sura replacement, but better. It weirded me out at first how easy it was talking about everything. I guess I had some practice with Sura, but Dexter just seems to understand it all, on another level. On a guy level. He gets how hard it is for me to even talk about this stuff. He's still not made fun of me at all, which is great, but also surprising. It's weird to spend so much time together without either of us filling the time with constant jokes.

My bedroom door opens suddenly and I jump a little, before remembering that I've finished the referral and already closed my laptop. Ma strides in, carrying a tray.

'I make you pakoras,' she says in stilted, awkward English. She smiles at Dexter as she puts the tray down on my bed.

I still can't help but cringe. Even though Dexter already met her when we got here after school, even though he said hello to her, and they had a semi-conversation. Just hearing her attempts at English makes me squirm inside, makes me nervous that Dexter is judging me, laughing inside his head at how dysfunctional my family is.

But instead Dexter grins with genuine delight. 'Oh my God these look amazing!' he enthuses.

I see the smile bloom on Ma's face in reaction.

'It made from onions and –'

'She means potatoes,' I tell Dexter. 'They've got potatoes and spices and some type of flour.'

Ma's face drops a little as she looks confusedly between Dexter and me. I shake my head at her as if to say, *It doesn't matter.*

'I bring ketchup too, for you, Ibrahim,' she says. I notice the bowl of sauce at the side of the plate of pakoras. I'm the only one in the family who eats them like this, drenched in ketchup. She remembered.

'Thank you, Mrs Malik,' Dexter says, picking up a pakora and then immediately dropping it back onto the plate and blowing on his fingers.

'Be care!' Ma says, alarmed.

God, why does she even bother trying if she can't say the right thing?

'They just look too inviting,' Dexter chuckles.

Ma's face creases in confusion.

'He means they look too good to wait,' I explain to her in Bengali. I instantly cringe again, because it's the first time I've

219

spoken Bengali in front of Dexter. I glance at him, expecting him to be laughing, but he's too busy blowing on a pakora, trying to cool it down. Of course he doesn't care. He's shown that he's a nice guy, a great friend, time and time again, but I just can't seem to get that in my head. He's seen the darkest parts of me now, surely the fact that my parents can't speak fluent English is nothing compared to him seeing me about to throw myself off a bridge.

Ma's face returns to a smile as she understands Dexter's compliment. She gives us both one last glance, says an awkward 'thank you' to us both and leaves the room. I feel myself relax as soon as the door closes.

'Sorry about her,' I say to Dexter, running a hand through my hair and tugging.

'Sorry for what?' he asks, pausing from trying to cool the food to look at me.

'Just, y'know.' I shrug, gesturing to where she was standing. 'She's awkward, innit?'

'At least your mother isn't dead,' Dexter says completely seriously.

I pause a second, looking at his serious face, waiting to see if he's joking or not. His mouth twitches a little and I shove his arm, making him drop the pakora.

'Don't take it out on my food!' he says, picking it up from where it dropped on my bed. He tests it on his lip, but realises it's still too hot.

'Doesn't matter how awkward someone is,' he says, 'if they're bringing you amazing home-made snacks. She even remembered to bring you ketchup. That's sweet of her.'

I take one from the plate and dip it into the bowl of ketchup. 'Try it my way,' I say. 'It'll cool it down a bit too.'

'So you gonna tell her?' he asks, copying me with the ketchup. 'About the referral and everything going on?'

'No,' I say immediately. 'My parents wouldn't understand. And anyway, I think it's better if I sort of get a handle on it first before talking to them about it, y'know? I'm only just starting to understand it properly myself. God knows if I'll ever be able to tell them about the . . . dark stuff though. It's such a hard thing to talk about. Especially with family, y'know?'

'Yeah, sure, these conversations are hard,' Dexter says, mouth full of pakora. 'But things will be better after it, trust me. Things have been great with Dad since our chat about Mum.'

'Yeah but that's *your* dad,' I say. 'My parents are . . . Well, you saw how awkward my mum is. Dad's the same. He said we'd talk about the comedy stuff, but that never happened.'

'Why don't *you* bring it up?'

I shake my head. 'I think it worked out for the best that he forgot, actually. I don't think I'm ready yet. I meant what I said about getting a handle on things myself first. I'm worried if we talk about it now, I'll just cave.'

'But you're not gonna give up stand-up, right?!'

'No way,' I say emphatically. 'I told them how much it meant to me, so at least they know that now. It's just about me remembering to think about my own needs as well as all the crap that they dump on me.'

'Good on you, mate,' Dexter says. 'You can't keep all that stand-up talent to yourself. The world of comedy needs you!'

'I just wish they could understand it, y'know? That they

weren't so clueless and understood that stand-up can be a proper career.'

'You're way too down on them, man,' Dexter says. 'You keep saying how awkward they are, but they're just like any other parents. My dad does the exact same thing when you come round. The cringey attempts to make conversation, the weird hovering thing parents like to do.'

He's right. I look at the tray of food in front of us, and remember Mr Murgen doing something similar when we were at Dexter's the other day.

'It's not just that though,' I say, going to tug on my hair, but then remembering I've got oily pakora hands. 'It would be fine if that was all it was. But it's like I told you on the bridge – they just . . . they don't behave like parents. There's so much I have to do for them that they should be able to do themselves. It's like I'm the parent and they're the kids a lot of the time.'

'Hmm,' he says, mouth still full. 'Well, then . . . why not just treat them like that?'

'Huh?' I ask, popping a whole ketchup-soaked pakora in my mouth. 'You reckon I should tell them off and send them to bed with no dinner?'

He rolls his eyes. 'I mean, like, teach them how to do things themselves, rather than just doing it for them. The way you taught Mariyam how to tie her own laces so you didn't have to do it any more. Just try the same sort of thing with your parents.'

'I get what you're saying, but it's just . . . I just . . . I shouldn't *have* to, y'know? I mean, they're the ones who should be teaching *me*, not the other way round. It's just . . . frustrating. Like, I bet you've never had to teach *your* dad anything.'

'Dude, do you not remember when he got obsessed with trying to mirror his phone to the TV, and I had to walk him through it step by step just so he could watch his lame coupon-spending show on the big TV?'

I laugh, remembering how Mr Murgen had accidentally projected his phone screen too early, and Dexter and I got a glimpse of his Notes app, which had a list of super cheesy self-affirmations for him to recite in the mornings. ('Put on your positivi-T-shirt . . . I believe in my dreams . . . I am doing my best, and that's always enough . . .')

'Mum used to say something,' Dexter says quietly. 'Once, after that time she got a ticket because she didn't know you couldn't drive in the bus lanes, and I teased her about it, she told me that even adults don't have their shit figured out. That they're just learning as they go too. Batshit, innit? They're supposed to be in charge, and yet they're as clueless as we are.'

'Uh, speak for yourself,' I say instinctively.

'And don't forget, yours is an extreme situation,' Dexter says, ignoring me. 'Your parents came over from a whole 'nother country, barely able to speak the language, not knowing how things work here. There wasn't anyone really to teach them, y'know? It must have been hard.'

'You're right,' I say. 'I feel bad complaining when I think about what they've been through.'

'No, don't!' he says quickly. 'Don't feel bad about being, like, unhappy, or stressed, or whatever. Just because there's a reason for something being bad, doesn't mean it doesn't still suck.'

'It's just, like . . .' I start, then look at him, getting the feeling that he's probably fed up of my whining by now. That maybe I've said too much already. But he's just looking at me, waiting, no impatience on his face. 'The whole teaching thing . . . Most of the time it's just easier and quicker to do it myself, y'know? Like, I've shown Dad a million times how to reset the broadband router. It's literally just pushing one button and waiting, but he *always* forgets how and calls me, or panics when it doesn't work instantly. It's honestly easier and quicker for me to do it myself.'

'Yeah, but then the vicious cycle continues, innit?' Dexter straightens up a little, the way he does when he's trying to be serious. 'I noticed it earlier actually, with your mum. She can totally speak enough to hold a basic conversation, but you just . . . you keep jumping in and speaking on her behalf and, like, I get it. Well, I mean, obviously I can't *really* get it, but I understand where you're coming from, but, like, it was as if you weren't even giving her a chance, y'know? It's sort of what my mum used to do, actually. Every time I struggled with something, she would just do it for me. It's why I still always wear slip-on shoes. Laces are hard, man.'

'You can't do laces?' I ask with a smirk. 'How can you do two different types of tie knot but can't do shoelaces?!'

He rolls his eyes. 'Well, I would be able to if my mum hadn't just always jumped in and done it for me. If she'd taught me the bunny method like you taught Mariyam.'

'I'll teach you if you want, little bunny,' I say, poking him in the side. 'Anyway, since when did you become an expert in all this shit? Seriously?'

He shrugs, takes another pakora and takes a bite without

dipping it in ketchup. 'Dad found this grief counsellor for me. She's helping me learn to deal with stuff.' His face begins to redden and he starts making little gasping noises, eyes wide, looking for his drink.

'Maybe he should find you a counsellor who can help you deal with spice,' I laugh, handing him his glass of water from the tray.

He guzzles the drink, his face getting redder and redder. I can't help but think maybe his solution is in fact the best way forward. To get my parents to stop relying on me so much, I need to get them to the stage where they can do the things themselves. And he's also right about the fact they never had anyone to teach them about the way things are here. I mean, they came over all alone, no family here at the time, didn't speak the language. It must have been really hard for them. I guess I could be a bit more patient, find a way that works best for them. I guess I need to adapt too.

39

Summer holidays are in full swing and things have been progressing nicely since that night on the bridge. I'm not going to pretend it's been, like, a miraculous change, where everything magically became OK because I reached rock bottom. There have been days since then that I've had panic attacks, had the bad thoughts, but I'm learning. I'm growing. I'm making an effort.

I'm actually running late to make that effort.

'Mariyam!' I call up the stairs. 'Hurry up! We're gonna be late!'

'Almost done!' she calls back.

I roll my eyes, and get her shoes out of the cupboard, lay them on the floor waiting for her, because I know that when she says 'almost done,' she is nowhere near done.

I check my watch. There's no way we're going to make it on time. Mariyam's going to ruin the surprise.

'Ibrahim!' Ma calls from the living room. I automatically clench my fists, the anger flaring up, knowing she's going to ask me to do something that'll make me even later. My brain fills with annoyance at having parents like mine who can't seem to do anything on their own.

But no. I need to interrupt this thought spiral. That's what the therapist who assessed me for my well-being referral called it. It was a . . . weirdly cathartic conversation. I was nervous as fuck at first. I thought the therapist would laugh at me, say I was exaggerating, that some people have it much worse and I should be grateful, but she did the opposite. She made me realise that this isn't all in my head. I mean, technically it is, obvs, but, like, I'm not an idiot for feeling like this. It made my struggles seem legit, and that was . . . just wow. She recommended me for a CBT class that starts next week. It's supposed to teach you how to manage your anxious thoughts. I literally burst out laughing when I heard the classes were going to be at the community centre. The woman probably thought I was having a breakdown, but it was just the coincidence of it all. Maybe in some way Sura will be able to see me in there, building on the stuff she taught me, finally talking about my problems in the real world, actually trying to fix things rather than just putting up with them.

Speaking of Sura. I haven't seen her again. I guess that was her goodbye on the bridge. I've been to the community centre a bunch of times since and there's been no sign of her. It made me sad at first. I do miss her. But mostly I want to thank her for everything she did for me. But then maybe she already knows, considering she's . . . like, magic. I guess she was only there for the hardest part, the lowest points. Maybe now that I've made the decision to get help, actually spoken to a therapist, like she so wanted me to, she's done her job and gone back to wherever she was when she wasn't helping me.

Remembering what she said, and what the therapist said on

the phone, I force myself to take a deep breath before going to see what Ma wants. I find her standing by the window, looking at her phone, waving it about in front of her face.

'What's wrong?' I ask her. I try to keep the irritation at being delayed out of my voice.

'I need to do my homework,' she says, still waving the phone around. It's on selfie mode and I can see her frowning face in the small screen.

'Homework?' I ask, confused.

'From that class your father and I went to at the community centre. They gave us some homework to do, but I can't get the camera to work properly.'

Dexter found this course for my parents. It's supposed to help South Asians navigate life in the UK; they do English lessons, help people learn how to fill in forms, how to use technology, all that stuff. Ma and Baba were both super up for going, which surprised me, but I guess I underestimated them again. I'm sort of annoyed at myself for not finding the class for them earlier. If they'd done it years ago, things could have been so much better now.

But no. I interrupt that thought spiral too.

'What do you need to do?' I ask her. I go to take the phone from her, but she yanks it away from me.

'No, no, I want to do it. Just tell me what button to press.'

'To do what? What's the homework?'

'I need to take a photo of my chilli plant and send it to the teacher on her email. But the camera isn't turning around. Do I need to do it like this?' she asks, spinning around to take a selfie with the chilli plant.

'Just push that button at the bottom,' I tell her, trying to stifle my laugh. 'It'll swap to the back camera.'

She scrunches up her face in concentration and taps the screen with her index finger in the way that old people use touchscreens. After a second she lets out a little squeak. 'What—?' she says, confused. 'Now it's made me look like a cat! I'm not a cat!'

I peer over to look at her screen and burst out laughing. She's somehow put a filter on that's given her cat ears and whiskers. Mixed with her confused expression, it looks hilarious.

I reach over and turn the filter off for her. 'It's that little button in the corner with the camera you need to turn it around.' I go to press it for her, but then remember what Dexter said about teaching rather than taking charge. 'Try it,' I tell her.

She gives me a look, then reaches over with her index finger and taps the button. She lets out a little squeal of delight when her chilli plant appears on the screen.

'Ah, OK,' she says, which is the Asian parent version of thank you.

The door to the living room opens and I turn around to find Mariyam standing there, hands on her hips, frown on her face.

'You can't tell me off for not being ready when *you're* not ready!' she says to me.

I roll my eyes. 'I was just helping Ma. You got everything?'

She shows me her backpack, which has a large piece of rolled-up paper sticking out of the top. She grins at me mischievously. 'Come on! We're gonna be late!' She walks over and grabs my hand with her newly uncasted arm and pulls me along.

* * *

The football match has already started when we get there, which is annoying but not the end of the world. At least the score is still nil–nil. Mariyam and I stop just before the crowd, and she swivels her backpack round and takes out our supplies. She's so giddy she can't stop giggling.

'Stop moving!' I chide, as I hold her chin with one hand, and the brush with the other. 'You're making me smudge the face paint.'

'Sorry,' she giggles. 'Are you drawing the flowers too? Or just the number five? I want some flowers.'

'But then Hamza won't see his number on your cheek if it's covered in flowers, will he?' I say, finishing the job.

'Hmm, OK then. But can we do flowers after?'

'Sure thing,' I say, using my phone as a mirror to paint Hamza's shirt number onto my cheeks too. 'You got your poster?'

She rolls out the giant piece of paper that reads 'GO HAMZA!' in bright red letters and grins at me.

'That's perfect,' I tell her. 'He's gonna love it. Make sure to hold it up high, yeah?'

She nods and begins to skip away towards the crowd. We manage to squeeze our way to the front, mostly down to Mariyam's cute squeaky voice calling out, 'Excuse me, please, small girl with a big poster for her brother coming through.' I love that she's so confident, so willing to make her place in the world.

When we're in view of the pitch, Mariyam holds her poster up as high as her arms will stretch and screams out, 'YAY,

HAMZA!' At the sound of his name, Hamza turns his head towards us. A look of confusion crosses his face, until I wave and Mariyam lets out an ear-splitting squeal. I wince at the sound, but notice the smile that spreads across Hamza's face as he sees us, sees the numbers on our cheeks, sees the poster Mariyam spent all morning making, realises that we looked up when his football match was so we could surprise him.

After this we'll go out for burgers, whether his team wins or not, and we'll sit and laugh together as siblings. I'll tell him in an awkward brotherly way that I'm proud he's doing something he enjoys, and that Mariyam and I will be at as many games as we can make from now on. That this will be our new tradition.

Then I'll make a joke to cut the tension, and Mariyam will want more chips, and Hamza will make her sing his praises in return for some of his.

It'll be perfect.

40

'Everyone having a good time?'

The crowd explodes into a deafening cheer. I wince a little, and see Dexter do the same, though there's a smile plastered across his face too.

'That's what I like to hear! Well, my name's Sophie, as most of you know.' A wolf whistle pipes up from the back of the room.

'Keep it in your pants, Matt!' Sophie calls out to the room of about thirty people. 'You've got no chance with me!' Everyone laughs and whoops.

I thought it would be super weird, coming to the stand-up club at Sophie's uni, thought everyone would look at me and Dexter, wondering why there were little kids running around campus. But everyone's been super nice, never once mentioned our age. They're all more focused on the comedy. The atmosphere here is electric, and Sophie is amazing as a host.

She ended up winning the community-centre competition. After Dexter and I (the other two in the top three) failed to show up, the prize money and mentorship went to Sophie by default. I'm not mad. The opposite really – thrilled that

I was good enough to finish in the top three. It's given me such a confidence boost. Made me realise that this is something I should carry on with, that I am actually good at this, despite what my anxiety sometimes tells me. I think Dexter was a bit disappointed about it in general, but like me, he wanted Sophie to be the one out of the rest of the contestants to win.

'We've got some fresh meat with us here today,' Sophie says, looking over to me and Dexter. A shiver runs through me as the crowd cheers for us. Part of me is terrified. Terrified that I'll get up there and have a panic attack, or that no one will find my material funny, that instead they'll jeer me off the stage, saying the standard here is way higher than in some pointless competition run by nobodies.

But I push away those thoughts by trying to find evidence to support them, and realising I can only find evidence against. I try and tap into the excited part of me instead, the part that's loved being on campus, loved seeing students who are as crazy about comedy as me get up on that stage to try out material and have fun. That's the thing about this. There's no scores, no points, no knockouts. People come here just to have fun. And most of the people watching are comedians themselves, so there's no one heckling, even the really drunk people. The atmosphere is just . . . nice. Friendly and encouraging. I feel at home. I feel like this could *be* my home, my future. I can picture Dexter and me sitting here after a day of lectures, winding down and supporting the new friends we'll make in this club.

'So, first up, everyone give a warm SkitHeads welcome to Ibrahim Malik, who's gonna share his talent with us tonight!'

The crowd breaks out into applause and cheers. People stamp their feet on the ground and start up a chant of my name. I legit almost tear up a little as I fist-bump Dexter. I can see he's feeling just as emotional as I am, being here, being able to do this. It's just . . . amazing. I try and savour the moment, while reminding myself that there's no pressure. I tell myself that if I get up on the stage and panic, I can make a run for it, and it won't matter because I never have to see any of these people again.

But I don't think that'll happen. I feel OK, walking up the steps. Nervous, obviously, but mostly in an excited way, rather than an anxious way. I've written a bunch of new material, all about mental illness and the stigma around it – particularly with men. I'm excited to see how it lands. The audience here knows what this moment feels like, getting up on the stage, trying something out for the first time. I think they'll be kind to me.

'Thanks, Sophie,' I say, taking the mic from her. I look out into the audience, the crowd of comedy lovers. My eyes land on Dexter. He mouths the words, 'You got this,' and gives me a thumbs up. Warmth radiates in me. I'm so grateful to have him. So grateful for his support, for his friendship. He told me earlier that he was proud of me. Normally, before all this, something like that would have made me feel super awkward. I would have cracked a joke about how mushy he was being and then changed the subject.

But not today. Today those words really struck me. I realised they're the words I've been waiting years for my parents to say. All my life, maybe. And while I'm still hoping the day comes where they feel like they *can* say that to me, it still means a lot that Dexter said it, that he feels that way. Perhaps it even means more that my best friend, the one who now knows me better than anyone, knows what I've been through, what it's taken to get me here, is proud of me. I focus on that feeling, that connection with him, as I take a deep breath and start my set.

'Hey, everyone. I'm Ibrahim Malik, and exactly two months ago I was about to throw myself off a bridge . . .'

SURA

'Would you like to introduce yourself?' the lady with the kind face asks.

They always have a kind face, though sometimes their words aren't as kind. I should know, with the amount of therapists and counsellors I've seen over the last three years. I've had all the sad head nods, the *hmm*s of pretending to understand, the repetitions of, 'This must be very hard for you.'

That sounds mean. Most of them *are* good. Most of them *have* helped. And I'm eternally grateful for that.

I stand up from my chair, everyone in the circle looking at me. I blur my eyes a little so I can't see them. I've learned that I'm able to speak more confidently if I do that.

'My name is Sura,' I say, tugging lightly at my headscarf. I wore my favourite bright blue one today; it always makes me more confident. 'I've done a bit of CBT before, and found it extremely helpful, so I'm here to just . . . refresh my knowledge a bit. I've . . . I've struggled with my mental health for years now, but it started to get particularly bad after my dad abandoned us.' A little murmur goes around the group, as it always does when I mention that. It comforts me in a way, to see that people agree that it's a big deal, that it's a valid reason for feeling the way I do.

One day I got home from school and he wasn't there. He'd taken all of his stuff, most of our money, and left my mum to look after me and my younger brother. And I know I should have been angry at him, but I was just . . . sad. So sad. Me and my dad had always been close. So when he left . . . it felt like it was my fault. Like I wasn't a good enough daughter, a good enough person, to make him want to stay with us. But then, so, yeah, my school had this counsellor I went to see, who really helped me reframe some of what I was feeling. But then . . . well, you were talking about the darkest point earlier, right? The event that triggers the idea that things are really not OK. Well, I can remember mine so clearly . . .

It was exactly one year after Dad left. Twelve months of waiting for him to come back, for him to realise what a mistake he'd made. To leave behind the new family he'd forged, according to the internet. The one with a stepdaughter my age. I was feeling super down after finding his new wife's profile, seeing all of that. And then just the knowledge that it had been a whole *year*, that he really wasn't coming back, and things would only get worse from then on . . . well, it got to me. A lot. I wanted to stay in bed all day, just looking over old videos and family photos and crying. But instead Mum dragged me to some distant relative's wedding.

I shouldn't have been surprised, really, that she had forgotten the one-year anniversary. Most of the time, it seems like I'm the only one in the family who actually remembers Dad existed. Nadeem I can excuse. He's only seven. But Mum? You'd think she'd care more. You'd think she'd remember the date, that she would be as affected as I was. But she didn't show any emotion, even when it first happened. Never once cried. At this wedding we went to, she just sat at a table with some other random aunties, laughing away about some gossip they were sharing.

That devastated me.

The wedding was being held at this fancy venue. It had a giant water fountain out the front. Nadeem was obsessed with it. Splashing in it, getting his suit wet, laughing so hard he got a stitch. There was also this balcony high up on the third floor, looking out over the grounds. I remember looking over the edge and all I could think about was jumping. Ending it all. All my thoughts were about how Dad left because of me, because I didn't do enough, wasn't good enough to make him stay, and that I should kill myself before I made things worse for Mum and Nadeem. I even formulated a plan as I stood on that balcony – to wait for everyone to go and wave off the bride at the gates and jump then. I was . . . so sure . . . that was the only way forward. The only way out. That was . . . that was the darkest moment.

But then . . .

I was just standing on that balcony, imagining the fall, wondering how much it would hurt. Wondering how quickly life leaves a body. How quickly we turn from a person into nothingness. Wondering what it would be like on the other side. Knowing that this would be such a huge relief. A way out from all the pain, and then . . .

'Sorry, excuse me?'

I turned to find a boy, about my age. He was staring at me, and I thought he might ask me if I was OK, might have realised what I was about to do. But instead he asked if I had seen his sister – a little girl in a bright pink shalwar khameez. I pointed her out to him; she was down in the fountain with Nadeem. The boy came closer, to look out over the edge like I was. He came right next to me and then . . .

I smelt him.

I smelt Dad.

Right away, memories flooded my mind of all the good times we'd had. When Dad and I went to the trampoline park together and I kept falling on him, and when I won the headteacher's award in Year 8 and he was so proud of me he hugged me the tightest he's ever hugged anyone. All those times I curled up in his lap as a child and fell asleep.

I legit started to feel dizzy. The boy noticed and asked me if I was OK. I lied and said I was. We both stood there and watched our siblings play together for a bit. Inside, I was begging the boy to leave. To take his (my dad's) aftershave with him and stop the images in my head, to stop the good memories overtaking the desire to jump.

But instead he started up a conversation. He told me all about his little sister, and how mischievous she was. Everything he

239

said about her made her seem just like Nadeem. It made me smile a little, feel a bit lighter.

Nadeem was . . . well, *is* . . . the most important thing in my life. Talking to this stranger, this boy who smelt like my dad, made me realise this. That it wasn't just me who had to cope with Dad leaving, so did Nadeem. And while Mum wasn't making any effort to make it easier for me, I could do that for him. I *should* do that for him.

I must have stopped talking or looked weird or something because the boy asked once again if I was OK. I turned and looked at him, saw true concern in his eyes. And then . . . a voice from below us shouted:

'Ibrahim!'
 I turned. The boy turned. He waved to his little sister. 'Hey Mariyam!'

'Ibrahim, the fountain is so cool!'

Ibrahim.

His name was *Ibrahim*.

Not only did he smell just like my father. He had the same exact name.

It was all so weird. Too much to just be a coincidence.

It was a sign.

We talked for a while. He told me how his sister always made him feel better when things were bad for him, and about how his brother was super annoying, but secretly a softie, and asked if I have that bond with my brother.

And the answer is . . .

Yes. Yes I do.

Nadeem and I have a bond. He's my everything. He makes things better when things are bad. He might have had to grow up without a father, but I was not gonna let him grow up with a dead sister.

I got super emotional then, and at the same time super embarrassingly my stomach let out a huge rumble. The boy didn't make fun of me. Instead he pulled out a napkin from his pocket, unravelled it and inside was . . . a samosa. He told me his little sister had asked him to carry it around for her in case she got hungry later, but that he thought I needed it more.

I don't know what it was about this. This tiny gesture of kindness. But I started crying, letting out all the emotions from inside me. It seemed to hit me all at once. This boy being there just when the dark thoughts were about to consume me. Him wearing the same aftershave as Dad, him having the same name. It all seemed like it was the universe sending me this huge sign. Telling me to change things before it was too late.

He didn't know to react. I think he tried to ask me if I was OK, but I felt super embarrassed so just ran away from him back into the hall.

It's my biggest regret. Running. Leaving him. I think about that moment so much.

That night I went and talked to my mum about it all. I told her everything, including what I nearly did, how much Dad leaving had affected me. She cried. I cried. Nadeem was asleep.

She got me help.
Proper help.
And that changed everything.
That boy . . . changed everything. He gave me a sign to carry on, that things could get better, to focus on the good in life. Without even meaning to, with a simple act of kindness, he gave me the will to live.

I've thought about that boy every day since we met. I sort of became obsessed with him. After I started therapy and taking antidepressants, and got back to feeling like myself again, I made it like my life's mission to find him. So that I could thank him. I still want to. I need to tell him how much that talk, that moment, that samosa meant to me. I need to thank him for saving my life.

But of course all I had to go on was his first name. And it's not exactly that unique a name, so I couldn't find him online anywhere, and trust me, I looked deep. I looked through the friend lists of all my cousins who were at that wedding, assuming that maybe he was a distant relative or something. And sure I found a bunch of Ibrahims, but none of them was him. I didn't know where he lived, what school he went to . . . nothing.

It seemed impossible, but he was ALL I thought about. Like, genuinely obsessed. I kept imagining the day we would meet again, when I'd be able to tell him how much he had helped me. I kept thinking of ways I could return the favour. Because I felt like that was the least I could do. He helped me so much, I needed to pay it back.

It's creepy, I know, but I used to dream about him too. Almost every night for a while. Each time we were in different scenarios where he needed help, and I managed to do it. I managed to make his life easier, or better, the way he did with me.

It's probably quite unhealthy how obsessed I am with this stranger. Though he doesn't feel like a stranger to me. It feels like I know him deeply. Like we're a part of each other. It feels like we're connected somehow.

I take a breath, after saying all this with practically no stops. I know I've probably shared too much. That this group of people will be thinking I'm a complete wacko, that Dad leaving really did mess me up, but it doesn't matter. I know that what I've said matters, and in turn that's *all* that matters.

There's a brief silence as I just stand there, trying to think what to say next, what else to say about myself, whether I should mention that I'd maybe like to teach CBT classes in the future. But then a woman in the group pipes up.

'So . . . did you find him?' she asks, practically falling off her chair in anticipation.

Before I can answer her, the door to the room opens with a small bang.

'Oh God, sorry,' the person entering says. 'Sorry I'm late, I just . . . I had a family thing, and then, well . . . yeah. Anyway, sorry again. It's . . . it's my first time.'

I blink.

Blink again.

No.
No freaking way.

Our eyes meet. He squints a little, pushes his glasses up his nose. And then his eyes light up. Surprise, then disbelief and then joy blooming on his face.

'Ibrahim?' I ask. 'Is it really you?'

The boy from the balcony – the boy who offered me a samosa and inadvertently changed everything, the boy who saved my life – smiles right back at me.

Resources

If you have been affected by any of the issues raised in this book, please consider reaching out to the organisations listed below.

Samaritans
Confidential emotional support for anyone in emotional distress, struggling to cope or at risk of suicide. Lines open 24/7.

Call free on 116 123 or visit www.samaritans.org

YoungMinds
Mental-health support for young people, including a free 24/7 text-messaging service.

For urgent help, text 'YM' to 85258 or visit www.youngminds. org.uk

Muslim Youth Helpline
Faith and culturally sensitive support by phone, live chat, WhatsApp or email.

Call 0808 808 2008 (4pm-10pm) or visit www.myh.org.uk

Acknowledgements

I never thought I'd have *one* book published, and yet somehow here I am writing the acknowledgements for my *third*. Dreams do come true, kids! (Still waiting for my pet peacock though . . .) As always, I would not have finished this book without a whole cast of helpers hiding behind the words.

Eternal thanks to my excellent editor Emma Matthewson for all her sage wisdom and patience while I figured out how to tell this story. To Talya Baker, the best copy editor in the world, for making me laugh while editing by pointing out how many times I overuse the word 'just', and questioning how much control the sun has over its actions. Thank you also to her talented daughter Sasha Baker for her eagle-eyed proofreading. (Picky word talent runs in the family!)

Thank you to everyone else at Hot Key for all you do. Shout-out to Sophie McDonnell for designing another fantastic cover. Also to Raj Dhunna for changing my mind about illustrated characters on book covers. It's always hard when someone else tries to manifest something you dreamed up, but Raj paid so much attention to detail, and managed to get all the key aspects of Ibrahim just right.

Ginormous thanks to my wonderful agent Hellie Ogden for continuing to put up with my never-ever-during-working-hours text messages and always knowing what to say to calm my silly brain.

Speaking of brains – CBT (cognitive behavioural therapy) isn't for everyone, but it truly changed my life. So much so that I wanted to write a book about it! Huge shout-out to those who work for the NHS Wellbeing Service (and the NHS in general!). In particular, humongous amounts of gratitude to Lauren Stenhouse who listened to hours of my nonsensical whining – including hits such as 'My lack of guilt makes me feel guilty', and 'No, trust me, I *do* know what they're thinking'. Thank you for giving me the tools to battle my very own Mildred.

Asking for help is always tough, but less so when you have an anxiety (totally the collective noun for a group of authors) of talented writer friends to hand. Shout-out in particular to Hanky Took and Nizrana Farook for the Zoom writing sessions, constantly pinging WhatsApp chats, and generally just for putting up with Stressed Yasmin. Thank you to Lucy Powrie and her inexplicably French autocorrect for always being a safe venting space that sometimes provides cute corgi pics. To Aisha Bushby for the constant reassurance, Katya Balen for always checking in and being jealous of whatever my mum is cooking that day, and Ryan Lynch for providing a Penis Opinion on this book when needed. Also to Sofia Saghir and Radiya Hafiza for their Brown People Perspectives, even when their experiences didn't line up with my book and I cursed them out (who knew Muslims weren't a monolith?!). Thanks to Sara Barnard for providing the harsh truths needed to develop myself as an actual author-type person and for easing me into life as a cat mum. Also shout-out to my cat, Islam. You're a bitey derp sometimes, but I adore you. (Now I've put you in my acknowledgements, will you start giving me cuddles??)

Thank you to the staff and students at Katherine Warington School for being super supportive and letting my imagination run wild in the library. It is an absolute privilege to be your librarian and be able to talk books as an actual job!

Lastly, huge thanks to my family, for everything. Special thanks to my brother Shamim for attending my award evenings and graduations, for celebrating my successes, buying me my first car, paying for the internet, etc., etc. You do far too much for us, and I'll never be able to properly articulate how much I appreciate it. Love you.

About the Author

Yasmin Rahman is a British Muslim born and raised in Hertfordshire. She has MAs in Creative Writing and Writing for Young People. Her debut novel, ALL THE THINGS WE NEVER SAID, was nominated for the Carnegie Medal, and was the runner-up YA book in the inaugural Diverse Book Awards.

Yasmin also works as a librarian at a secondary school, where she spends her days making funky displays and trying to shove her friends' books into students' hands. In her spare time, Yasmin watches every medical drama ever made, and sometimes designs bookish fan art; her posters are sold worldwide on behalf of John Green, and Colleen Hoover.

Also by Yasmin Rahman

Your friend or your secret –
which one will you keep?

Read on for an extract.

1

There are plenty of theories about the best way to wake up in the morning. Some go for a gradually brightening light alarm, waking up gently as they adjust to the fake sunrise. Others opt for loud noises that immediately strike fear in their heart. I, on the other hand, put forward that the most effective way to get someone out of bed is having their five-year-old brother sit on their head.

'Oh my God, Ismail, GET OFF!' I yell, my voice muffled by his body.

Ismail giggles as he wiggles around on my face. I can't help but laugh too as I push him off. He flops onto the mattress, cackling maniacally. I take my chance, reach over and start tickling him under the arms; as expected, he screams happily.

'Shhhhh,' I say, covering his mouth and watching the door. 'We'll get told off.'

Ismail's grin slowly melts against my palm.

'Why are you up so early?' I ask, reaching for my phone to check the time. The screen doesn't light up. I tap it again. Nothing. I press the power button and my stomach drops when I see the dead battery sign. I check my charger lead and find that it's been disconnected from the plug adapter all night.

'Oh crap,' I say, jumping out of bed. I check the clock on

the wall. 'We are *so* late,' I tell Ismail. His slightly too long black hair is standing up in haywire tufts, and his Spiderman pyjamas are all crinkled from the tickle fight. Ammi normally wakes him up and gets him ready; I don't understand what's happened today. I need to shower. Now I guess I'll need to get Ismail ready too. And give him breakfast. And, oh God, I was supposed to wake up early to revise for my biology practice exam! Crap, crap, crap.

'Where's Ammi?' I ask. I'm angry at her. My phone died during the night, but what's her excuse? She's meant to be up first. It's her job to do all this. Ismail is usually eating breakfast when I wake up.

'She's sleeping,' he tells me, casually stretching out across my bed. 'I tried waking her but she won't get up.'

She must be having an off day. She has these sometimes, where she can't get out of bed. I'll come home from school and she'll only just be eating breakfast. On days like this, things are super scattered, and it makes me anxious and flustered. Normally I'm up on time and can take over.

'OK, right,' I say, trying to gather myself. 'Right, yes . . . let's . . . We can do this. First things first, you need to get into your uniform.'

Ismail looks right at me and blows a raspberry, before dissolving into laughter again.

Oh God, this is going to be hard.

'I don't wanna eat Shreddies! I want pancakes!' Ismail says, knocking over the box of cereal so brown squares scatter across the table. I pick one up and pop it into my mouth, partly because they're delicious, and partly to stop myself from yelling, like I so want to. I don't know how Ammi does this every day; Ismail can be really annoying when you're stressed.

'We're already late – there's no time for pancakes,' I tell him, picking up the box and fixing the mess he's made. 'We don't even have time for breakfast, but I know you'll just end up cranky and your teacher will tell Ammi off again. Just eat your cereal. Here, I'll even put some sugar on it for you.' I go to sprinkle some sugar in his bowl, but he knocks the spoon out of my hand and starts giggling again.

'Ismail!' I yell. 'This isn't funny. We're *so* late. Can you just eat. Please?'

'No Shreddies! I want pancakes!'

Ughhhhhh. This boy, I swear to God. Sometimes he acts like he's three years old, not five. I look at the clock and panic again. I should've just given him a banana and forced him out of the door. I look down at his grinning face, those mischievous brown eyes, and realise I need to play dirty if I'm gonna get anywhere with him.

'Fine, you know what? You don't have to go to school today. At all,' I say.

His eyes light up and he sits up straight. 'For real?'

I nod, cleaning up the spilled sugar on the table. 'Yeah, you can just stay at home. Ammi's not well, so she'll be in bed all day. It'll just be you and Abbu when he gets back from work. I don't think he's gonna be happy about you skiving though.'

That does it. His smile drops. I almost feel bad, but I force myself to act normal. Calm. Like Ammi. I hand him the cereal spoon again. He takes it this time.

'Can I watch a video?' he asks, his mouth still empty. 'One of yours?'

I shouldn't let him; I know that it's a bad habit. But I also know the best thing to do right now is let him have his way. My phone's still on charge, so I grab Ammi's iPad, load up my YouTube channel and pass the device over.

Making videos is my biggest hobby. I make all kinds of weird things – remakes of movie scenes (mostly Disney films) using toys or household items, videos of Ismail being goofy, and sometimes stop-motion shorts. Ismail helps with a lot of them, which is probably why he's so into them. I usually save watching them as a treat for him, but like I say, this is an extreme case.

He *finally* starts eating, and I busy myself making cheese sandwiches for his lunch. God, I can't believe we woke up *this* late. As I spread mayonnaise, I imagine what will happen when I get into school. Miss Kirtley in reception is always a bitch to anyone who's late – 'You'll get nowhere in life if you turn up late, Amani,' she'll say. And then there's the whole thing of having to walk into class while everyone's already working. I'm tempted to skive, but like Ismail, the thought of being around Abbu all day while Ammi's upstairs resting is a bit much.

As if I've willed him into existence, I hear Abbu's voice. My heart spikes, thinking he's going to go ballistic, seeing Ismail and me still at home, seeing me making sandwiches while Ammi's asleep upstairs. I turn around, the butter knife almost dropping from my hand, but then I realise that Ismail has just switched over to the live TV app on the iPad. And there's Abbu on the screen, smile plastered across his face. You'd think I'd be used to this by now – Abbu's been a presenter on a kids' TV show about vets and animals, *Creature Clinic*, for years, though I haven't watched it myself in ages. Today he's on adult TV though. Some breakfast show, trying to promote the next series of *Creature Clinic*.

'Look, Maani, it's Abbu!' Ismail says, his voice full of glee (and, thankfully, Shreddies).

We both watch the screen, watch this version of Abbu that we never see at home. I get that he has to become this personality for his job, but it's honestly like a completely different person is in front of me. He even has banter with the presenters as he sits on the sofa, stroking a cat. The presenters are also holding small animals. They're laughing as if they've never heard someone funnier than Abbu. It makes me smile – seeing that he's so good at his job.

Abbu was a proper vet for years, when I was younger, and then he got offered the *Creature Clinic* gig, which paid a lot more. He often does these live TV appearances to promote the show – he'll go on and entertain people with some cute animals and weird facts.

I focus on putting extra mayonnaise on Ismail's sandwiches because I know he likes them soggy. I'm just cutting the crusts off when I hear yelling from the iPad. I turn to find chaos on the screen. Everyone is up off the sofa now. There's a . . . a cat attached to Abbu's beard. He tries to shake it off, but it's got a death grip on him. The blonde female presenter screams as his movements make the cat swing back and forth. Next thing I know, the other animals have gone berserk too. There's a lizard tangled in the blonde lady's long hair, with the same death grip, and a guinea pig runs into the audience.

'Get this fucking piece of shit off me!' Abbu yells, as the woman continues to scream.

He stumbles and falls backwards over the sofa. There's a loud crash and then all you can see is his legs sticking up behind the red sofa.

The screen *finally* cuts to the weather.

I am mortified. Ismail, however, is cackling. Milk-running-from-the-corners-of-his-mouth, danger-of-choking-type cackling.

'Did you see that, Maani?' He turns to me, tears in his eyes. 'Abbu had a cat on his face! He fell over!' He begins cackling again.

Oh God, this is bad. So bad. Fear courses through my body. Abbu is going to feel . . . humiliated.

'Ismail, come on,' I say, more fiercely than ever. 'We have to go. Now.' I snatch up the half-finished bowl of cereal and drop it in the sink.

'Hey, my Shreddies!'

'Oh, *now* you want them?' I shove his sandwiches into his lunch bag.

'I want Ammi,' he says, a slight whine in his voice.

I don't reply, just focus on filling his water bottle.

'Why is she still sleeping?' he asks. 'Isn't she gonna walk me to school?'

'Nope, it's gonna be me today.'

We need to leave. Need to get away from here as soon as possible. I keep seeing Abbu falling backwards over the sofa, the cat attached to his beard.

'Get your shoes on.'

'But Ammi *always* walks me to school,' he says, still at the table. 'She's walked me before when she's sick. Why not today?' He's talking in that soft vulnerable voice that says he's about to start crying. Oh God, it's breaking my heart.

'Hey, it'll be fun. Just us two. We can blow dandelions on the way. Sound good?' Ismail loves doing this in the garden.

'Will Ammi pick me up?' he asks, looking up at me.

'What, I'm not good enough for you?' I joke.

'I want Ammi to take me.'

I can hear the tears crawling further into his voice. No no no! It's at times like this I wish Ismail could suddenly be five years older. I love him to bits, but he can be a handful to look after, even more so when I'm already stressed about being late, about my biology practice exam, about Abbu, and Ammi, and just everything. I *need* to get to school. There's something about school that calms me. Even though I'm not the best student, I like being there. At school, I know what's happening. I know what classes I'm supposed to be in, where I have to go next. I know what we're going to be learning about, and the names of everyone in my class. There's structure, and certainty. Ten times ten is always one hundred. But at home . . .

'Hey, c'mon, don't be sad,' I tell Ismail, immediately cringing because I know this will make it worse. As expected, the tears start falling.

'Wanna know something *super fun* we can do?' I ask him, desperately trying to both distract and cheer him up. 'I can take you the super-secret way to school. No one knows about this way. Not even Ammi.'

'Really?' he sniffles. 'But Ammi knows everything.'

'Not this. This is a secret only I know. It's the big-kid way.

And today I'll let you in on it, but you have to promise not to tell anyone. I can trust you, right?'

He nods eagerly.

'Good, OK, now hurry up and put your shoes on – otherwise we won't have time to go the secret way.'

He scrambles into the hallway. Thank God.

Now I just have to think up some secret way to walk to school.